SIÂN PHILLIPS' NEEDLEPOINT

SIÂN PHILLIPS' NEEDLEPOINT

GUILD PUBLISHING
LONDON

To Robin, Kate, Pat and the boys

Photographs by Mike Martin
unless otherwise stated

Design and diagrams by Annette Stachowiak

This edition published 1987 by
Book Club Associates
By arrangement with Elm Tree Books/Hamish Hamilton Ltd

Typeset by Tradespools Ltd
Printed and bound in Great Britain by
William Clowes (Beccles) Ltd, Suffolk

Contents

Foreword *7*

The Development of Canvas Embroidery *14*

Basics *27*

The Essential Stitches *35*

Additional Stitches *40*

Left-Handed Needlepoint *53*

Samplers *57*

Projects and Sources of Ideas *67*

Your Own Canvas Start to Finish *83*

Some Guidelines on Colour *95*

Frames or Not... *100*

Finishing *108*

Putting Things Right *117*

Appendix *123*

Acknowledgements *126*

Useful Books *127*

Index *128*

NAMING

Some people call canvas embroidery 'tapestry'. It is also referred to as 'needlepoint' and 'petit-point' and 'gros-point'. Which is it?

Well, it isn't tapestry for a start (though 'tapestry work' might qualify – just). Tapestry is made by weaving: a very different process from that of embroidering, and the pattern is *in* the fabric (one could say, it *is* the fabric).

Embroidery is worked *on* a fabric; the design is imposed but because canvas embroidery can look remarkably like tapestry, people began making the mistake of calling it 'tapestrie' as far back as the seventeenth century. Human nature being what it is, it would be surprising if some upwardly mobile Tudor hadn't tried to pass off a bit of embroidered arras as the rather grander tapestry, which it so resembled.

To add to the confusion, in America canvas embroidery has nearly always been called 'needlepoint' and that term is often extended to cover any embroidery that involves counting threads.

'Petit-point' and 'gros-point' continue the muddle. One would imagine petit-point to refer specifically to very fine work, but in fact it means tent stitch, small, medium or large in size, depending on the size of canvas on which it is worked. Gros-point is cross stitch and again, the size of the stitch is regulated by the base fabric.

The only correct term is 'canvas work' or 'canvas embroidery', but because I'm used to it and because I love the needlework I've seen done by Americans, I also shall call it 'needlepoint'.

FOREWORD

Strange as it may now seem, time was when girls aspiring to be Business Woman of the Year or Girl-best-acquainted-with-the-works-of-Wittgenstein recoiled nervously from showing any aptitude for the skills traditionally deployed by mother and grandmother. It was as though a deft hand with skillet or needle marked one out as being unsuited for the great, emancipated world which one somehow had to learn to inhabit.

My aspirations were relatively modest: all I wanted was to be a single lady doing nothing except acting and filling in my leisure hours by going to acting classes, voice classes, dancing classes and going to the theatre to watch other people acting. (Life didn't turn out like this, except in patches.) I remember feeling quite pleased when I was thrown out of my needlework class and told that I'd better try my hand at a bit of carpentry. It seemed to underline the fact that I had all the makings of a late '50s version of the New Woman. It shames me to recollect that I used to sit swinging my legs reading Shakespeare while everyone except one other recalcitrant cousin steamed away getting in the hay.

This New Woman, grown up and having to join the human race, had a horrible time serving inedible meals and having to pay 'little women' to mend clothes and turn sheets. She not only couldn't cook or sew or garden, but she'd also neglected to learn how to change a washer or mend a fuse. During a period of penury, learning to cook well became an urgent necessity, and now cooking – if not always well – is an abiding pleasure. Gardening – well, any sort of outdoors labour – came upon me quite suddenly and unexpectedly and has remained an obsession. Sewing came harder. In fact, it didn't come at all. I had to creep up on it, and even now I can't sew a fine seam. Fortunately, there are other things one can do with needle and yarn . . .

Had I possessed half the sense I was born with, or had I not evolved such a narrow view of 'culture', I could have learned so much at the feet of the women who raised me. As it is I've had to put on great spurts of effort trying to catch up with my past.

My grandmother, Elizabeth George, later 'Mrs Thomas, Tŷmawr', was such an exquisite plain needlewoman that people would say, 'It is worth wearing a hole in your sock to have one of Mrs Thomas' darns on it.' (This in Welsh.)

When I fell in love with Robin, my husband, I bore away a cashmere sweater of his thinking what an original gift an exquisite darn would be . . . It took me a week to produce something really horrible and he bought a new sweater. My frugal soul enjoys mending but the results are nothing one would wish to inspect.

Mother, 'Sally, Tŷmawr', was a superb knitter. Not only was she technically expert but her original designs were quite extraordinary for someone who was so busy teaching that, for her, clothes were no more than 'decent covering'. Bearing in mind a romantic recollection of Mummy with needles stuck in her hair, one between her teeth and several in the knitting, I thought I would make Robin a cable-knit sweater. Having whisked through Patricia Roberts' shop and bought a lot of mohair wool I went off on location to Ireland and started knitting in the intervals of filming. Two weeks later, Marie Kean, who was playing Sean O'Casey's mother (I was playing Countess Markowitz) and who was entertaining me in the country for the weekend, saw a large tear trickle down my cheek as I began to unpick the spoiled work for the umpteenth time; she seized the whole thing and threw it on the fire. Thank God for a woman of resolve. I brought the remaining wool back to my mother-in-law, Eleanor Summerfield. At the time she was in a long West End run and in a twinkling in her dressing room she had produced a wonderful mohair sweater for *me*. (Not only highly numerate but a wise ma-in-law.)

On my rare excursions into the High Life I used to visit surely one of the most beautiful women in the world, and one of the nicest, Silvana Mangano, while she summered in the south of France. We took to each other, although my Italian and her English were sort of basic. As Signora de Laurentiis she had to entertain all sorts of people – some quite horrid, I thought – who descended on the south of France in shoals each day, hoping to talk 'deals' with her husband. I admired her poise and calm as she sat looking exquisite in her salon while the butler served one-only-but-perfect drinks. Sitting under a pretty antique lamp in the dying sunlight she would nurse a martini, saying virtually nothing, and doing – what? Well, now I know she had a defence against all those incomprehensible and voluble Californian gentlemen. She was doing incredibly complicated needlepoint. At the time it was a mystery to me.

Foreword

These chairs, sewn in basketweave stitch, were made by Silvana Mangano for Terence Stamp and were begun when they were filming Theorem in 1969. They took four years to complete. Silvana is a perfectionist in all she does, but even so I was astonished when Terence revealed that all the out-of-sight bits are embroidered – underneath the seat cushions and the against-the-wall back of the chairs!

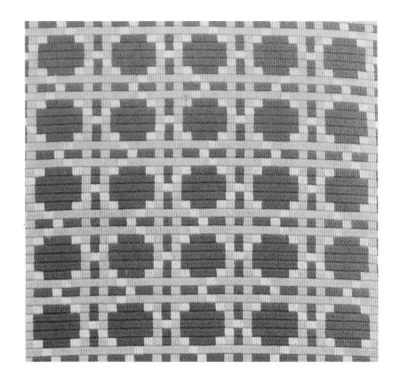

Wonderful actress and actor-manageress and one of
my dear chums till her death, Marie Löhr was not
what one could call good with her hands – in the
handiwork sense, that is. On stage they spoke
volumes. During a period in her illustrious life when
the butler, the chauffeur, the Rolls and the launch
were removed she found it necessary to learn to cook
(mainly Steak Diane as far as I could perceive) and
since she was an inveterate gift-giver she learned to
crochet lovely circular shawls. I took lessons for six
weeks backstage at the Garrick Theatre before she
suggested that in my case it might be cheaper and
quicker to buy shawls from Harrods.

An aunt left me some exquisite quilts. Mother gave
me some beautiful damask and lace tablecloths
worked by a cousin. I acquired a cousin-in-law who
worked a sampler which was rather better than
grandmother's. I began to feel hopeless about my

Coral Browne

ability and rather closed my mind to the subject and got on with things I *could* do with my hands: wielding a pick-axe, building dry-stone walls and grubbing out tree roots.

Imagine my indifference when Coral Browne, who had battled her way through several weeks of rehearsal wreathed in my cigarette smoke, narrowed her beautiful eyes, tapped one exquisitely shod foot and pronounced that a way of improving the quality of life (hers) and prolonging it (mine) was to introduce me to canvas embroidery.

Strong *men* tend to obey Coral, and convinced though I was that yet another humiliating debâcle lay just round the corner, I meekly took myself off to the Women's Home Industries shop in Pimlico to buy wool, needles and a beautifully prepared canvas.

Six hours later I was an addicted canvas embroiderer, making mistakes surely, but I could see that I was going to be able to *do it*. And that it was going to look stunning. Half way into my first cushion (pillow) I was feverishly devising grandiose projects (I firmly believe that Thinking Big makes any activity more interesting). Veils have to be drawn over the virtues of canvas embroidery as a cure for smoking. It took the combined efforts of Burgess Meredith, Paul Rogers and a hypnotherapist to stop my mad career as a nicotine addict and that was many years later.

However, even then, in the '60s, chain-smoking and dropping bits of ash all over my chest (not the beautiful image conjured up by 'embroidery', 'tapestry', 'needlework', 'needlewoman'), I was exhilarated to realise that I had finally found something which I, with few skills, could do quite beautifully. Fairly soon I was finishing a small 'carpet' (hearth-rug more like) and I realised that I was, against all expectations, joining the shades of my grandmothers and aunts and mother.

Rapidly over-dramatising I could see the whole thing:
    'And what is that wall-hanging, Miss O'Toole?'
    'Oh, that's something Mummy did years ago.'
    'How interesting to think that life must have been
so leisurely in the 1970s and '80s'.

The Development of Canvas Embroidery

If, knowing nothing of the technique of canvas embroidery, you were to take a stout needle and thick yarn and contemplate a piece of coarse but evenly woven fabric with a view to decorating it, the odds are that you would eventually find yourself making stitches that vertically and diagonally crossed the intersection of the vertical and horizontal threads (the *woof* and the *warp*). You would, in effect, be doing the simplest possible thing: making half-cross or tent stitch. From this it would be a short step to the full cross, and you might even find yourself counting the threads in order to make groups of these stitches. There really is a pleasant quality of inevitability about the stitching of canvas embroidery. When people began gardening, cooking, making pots and decorating them, and weaving cloth, they also felt the urge to decorate the clothes they wore and there are remnants of peasant embroidery from very early times.

We know that the Romans did canvas embroidery (or something very similar) and there are examples of late Anglo-Saxon sewing in the same manner. The slight difference in appearance from present-day needlepoint is accounted for by the fact that the 'canvas' background is a *fabric* coarse enough to enable the embroiderer to part the vertical and

The Syon Cope – a fine example of Opus Anglicanum *(photo courtesy of the Trustees of the Victoria and Albert Museum, Crown Copyright).*

horizontal threads, and not canvas as we know it where the spaces (or holes) are very clearly presented.

Opus Anglicanum is the name given to the first great period of English embroidery. The golden age of the thirteenth century saw English work, both ecclesiastical and secular, avidly sought after and treasured, foremost in beauty and importance throughout Europe. The gold and silver threads and the precious and semi-precious stones incorporated into the designs of church vestments and the garments and rich ornaments worn by the nobility (and their mounts) made the embroidery an excellent business proposition and many of the major pieces were commissioned as a very worthwhile investment. The Syon Cope which can be seen at the Victoria and Albert Museum in London dates from this period and would have been sewn by teams of professional embroiderers, men as well as women, who qualified for such work only after many years of apprenticeship.

This kind of work continued for the next few centuries and many factors contributed to its eventual decline in quality and importance: political unrest in Europe; widespread and virulent contagious diseases; limited travel, commerce and exchange of ideas. Also, silks from Europe became available in Britain while our textile industry lagged behind and the embroidery, which had already lost its pre-eminence, gradually became less complex as the embroiderers struggled to compete with the easier-to-produce yet sumptuous fabrics.

It is not until the sixteenth century and the advent of the Tudors that we arrive at the next high-water mark in the story of English embroidery. At this stage what we refer to today as 'canvas embroidery' emerged. Canvas proper was now used as a base and there developed an emphasis on canvas work as an important domestic activity undertaken by amateurs as well as by the professional 'imbroiderers'. These professionals were resident in wealthy homes and employed on a full-time basis, or travelled from great house to great house, as did designers and artists. It is often said that one could enjoy travelling back in time only if one could travel back *rich* . . . This is never truer than of the Tudor period. Imagine having a back-room full of people doing all one's counting and measuring and sewing all the boring bits!

It is easy to see why everything in sight in a big Tudor house was richly embroidered. Just think of those huge windows: it must have been a nightmare trying to achieve some warmth. Then the floors – stone and bare, or strewn with rushes. Furniture was minimal: wooden benches and stools and chairs which were not designed for lounging. Nothing was conducive to warmth and comfort, so soft furnishing, wall-hangings, bed-hangings and cushions were essential. (Queen Elizabeth is said to have spent a good deal of time sitting on cushions on the floor and that gives a fair indication of how elaborate they would have been.) Bearing in mind the intense love of beauty and avid interest in nature and in the arts that characterises the Tudors, it would have been natural for them to make these necessities of life sumptuous and beautiful, and ornamentation and embroidery made them stronger, more hard-wearing and more conducive to warmth. No fools they.

Clothes, as well, not only reflected status and taste, but had to play their part in keeping the wearers warm for the better part of a typical English year. One notices that clothes were layered (rather in line with modern thinking) and this, along with the almost unimaginable richness of the embroidery, must have helped insulate the wearers. This is a description of a *foreparte* worn by Queen Elizabeth: '. . . white satten embroidered all over very faire like seas, with dyvers devyses of rockes, shippes and fishes embroidered with Venise golde, sylver, and silke of sondrye colours, garnished with some seed pearle' – an indication of the scope of Elizabethan taste in decoration in general. Nor were they averse to incorporating decoration from another age into their contemporary schemes when, after the Reformation, what ecclesiastical embroidery was not destroyed found its way into noble houses, and, cut up and adapted, added to the general splendour of hangings and cushions.

It is interesting to note that I felt moved to remark that men, as well as women, were embroiderers during the thirteenth and fourteenth centuries. Within a hundred years there was no longer equal pay for equal work (with women at the disadvantage) and, by Tudor times, there is reference only to professional male embroiderers. The famous designers and teachers were also men. Women must have been involved, but they are not much talked of and the decline of the professional woman embroiderer culminated in her exclusion from the emerging Guilds of the sixteenth century. However it is at this point that we encounter for the first time our true 'ancestors': the amateur embroiderers who must have been greatly helped in their work by the first appearance of books of designs and by the availability of herbals and bestiaries (still a rich source of designs). You can imagine the impact of the metal needle in the 1560s. I have never tried using a bone needle of the kind that was in use until that time, but I would guess that you would have had to be very nimble and skilled and patient to turn out fine work – and a lot of it. Most importantly, the new amateur embroideress was noble and had the means to employ good artists to draw and paint designs.

A great deal is known of the domestic arrangements of Bess of Hardwick, the Countess of Shrewsbury, one of whose husbands (she was an enterprising marrier) was for a time gaoler to Mary, Queen of Scots. Bess and Mary collaborated on several projects and Bess produced and accumulated huge quantities of canvas embroidery. In all probability ladies worked alongside professionals in a room set aside for embroidery and anyone who could be spared from other duties would be expected to lend a hand, so the output would have been continuous and steady. (Bess doesn't sound like the sort of person who would be pleased to see anyone taking a bit of time off.)

Queen Elizabeth was also an embroiderer, and it's comforting to note that the only cushion that she signed has a reverse side which no-one could call neat!

The designs of this period vary enormously. Large, bold rooms with ornate plasterwork and heavy oak furniture demand large, formal designs and these look magnificent, but there is also a charming informality about many of the designs. Teeming with life and vitality, little figures jostle with birds and beasts and are adorned with sometimes improbable flowers and plants, drawn from herbals as well as from books of designs.

Shortly after I began embroidering I, as I thought, stumbled upon a very effective way of reducing labour without losing impact and that was to embroider narrow strips and small pieces of needlepoint and then to appliqué them on to a large piece of cloth. It's an effective way all right. It's also

The 'pheasant' detail from the Oxburgh Hangings, described as a Maryan example; that is, the work of Mary, Queen of Scots (photo courtesy of the Trustees of the Victoria and Albert Museum, Crown Copyright).

hundreds of years old and was used to stunning effect in the sixteenth century, when small pieces or strips of cloth were embroidered and applied to damask or velvet and the edges oversewn with threads of gold and silver. Late in the century when Oriental carpets made their appearance in England it is to be imagined how they were prized. Then, as now, unusual and imported objects were displayed as a sign of status and property, but they also provided a new source of ideas for native embroiderers who copied them in needlepoint. One of the most spectacular is the Bradford Table Carpet at the V & A.

The Tudor period is a lovely one. Canvas embroidery had all the confidence and brilliance of a medium which was established as supreme not only in usefulness but in comfort and beauty. The upholstery, bed hangings, pictorial panels, cushions, purses, all reflect the subtlety and endurance, and the high style and glamour of needlepoint at its best.

This undisputed supremacy couldn't last and in time needlepoint had to take its place alongside crewel work, or imported silks which became the rage for hangings. Very often hangings disappeared altogether as building practice 'softened'; oak gave way to finer wood like walnut. Canvas embroidery was still used extensively but one finds it used more and more for bits and bobs: frames, small bags, boxes, book covers and framed pictures. Heroic exceptions are the Hatton Garden wall hangings which were accidentally discovered in Hatton Garden, unharmed under layers of wallpaper. They are dated 1690 and were found in 1896. There are six panels, each 7 foot 9 inches by 4 foot, and worked in a rich variety of stitches: tent, cross, rococo satin, brick, rice, eye, Florentine and French knots. They are on view at the V & A and well worth a visit.

The eighteenth century saw a return to more 'useful' work and canvas-embroidered upholstery reached a climax of elegance (and a great deal of it has survived). Pastoral and biblical scenes were very popular and books of designs proliferated, though many ladies designed their own work. Even when designs were copied from books, colour and material remained the choice of the embroiderer and there are charmingly idiosyncratic combinations of widely differing styles of design. France led the field in design and fashion – and changed them each year; a foretaste of 'the Collections' ! There was an airiness and delicacy in interior decoration which demanded an equally light touch in the style of needlework, and flame stitch (or Florentine or Hungarian point or Irish stitch as it was called in the seventeenth century) complemented the elegance of the furniture. Of course, women were out and about more in a freer society, so the output of domestic embroidery was reduced and in many houses silk damasks prevailed as curtains and hangings. There was also a fashion which persists to this day and it's one which I find difficult to like. In the latter part of the eighteenth century the best known paintings of famous artists of all periods were painstakingly copied in needlework which was meant to look as much like painting as possible. One has to tip one's hat to the labour and skill involved but I cannot for the life of me see the point of the exercise, which seems to me to diminish both the subject matter and the excellence of the needlework.

This country changed utterly in the nineteenth century. The Industrial Revolution saw a huge shift of population from country to town (and a completely different living pattern) and the emergence of a new sort of woman: middle or lower middle class, educated along narrow lines, constrained by clothes and manners, with precious little to do at home and

An early eighteenth century English chair seat, worked in Hungarian point (photo courtesy of the Trustees of the Victoria and Albert Museum, Crown Copyright).

few outlets outside it. Canvas embroidery became an obsession!

Booklets of contemporary designs abounded and were much of a muchness. The resulting work was on the whole a bit dull. Then a rage seized the country for what was called Berlin work. It was so popular that it wasn't necessary to say 'needlepoint' or 'canvas embroidery', Berlin work *was* embroidery.

It seems odd but until this point no one had thought to produce printed, squared-paper *patterns* for canvas embroidery. A German husband and wife

combined the artistic and technical skills necessary and started a bumper business in patterns for decorative objects. The demand was tremendous. It was a case of piling decoration upon decoration: tablecloths sported borders and fringes and covered tables whose legs were clothed. Upholstered chairs were given needlework cushions and sat near embroidered foot-stools on embroidery carpets. There were embroidered tie-backs around embroidery-bordered curtains, edgings around chimney-pieces, picture frames, pictures themselves: copies of lithographs of stately ruins or illustrations from contemporary novels and lots of well-behaved animals, the royaler the better. The designs were painted on (later stamped on) to the canvas, the colours were pre-determined and a dreadful bright sameness (the new synthetic dyes were *very* bright) descended on the Victorian drawing-room and its master, who might of an evening be found wearing an embroidered floral waistcoat, slippers bearing foxes' heads and maybe a little smoking cap bearing embroidered pansies.

In fairness, as time passed, colours became softer and a restraining hand was placed on the rioting flowers.

One element of the work of this period which is quite rightly being re-explored is the incorporating into the needlework of 'foreign' elements: beads in china or glass or jet and bits of brass or cut-steel – agony of course when used on chair seats (as they were, can you believe?) but very interesting when judiciously deployed.

To be even more fair, many pieces of Victorian canvas-work are lovely, taken singly; I have a great fondness for the carpets with their huge, overblown flowers, those little posies with trailing ribbons and the small dogs, seated on their cushions. It is, all the same, easy to sympathise with the reaction against these 'futile pictures', 'monuments of misplaced activity' and over-heated 'objets'. The reaction, when it came, was radical. It was not against the embroidery especially, but the influence of the 'modern' world was deeply felt in every aspect of life.

So what happened next? It is easy to look back, as I have been doing, and to note how nicely styles and fashions break down into half centuries, centuries or decades. In reality, course, they don't behave anything like as tidily. Anything to do with human beings is infinitely more muddled, and making sense of one's own time or that of one's mother is beyond the talent of a layman. The best I can do is to make a few observations and hazard a few guesses.

Towards the end of the Victorian era, needlepoint declined in popularity. It was inevitable that, with the advent of William Morris and all that one associates with him and the New Arts and Crafts Movement, Berlin work should collapse and disappear. Add to that the re-defining of the role of women; the simplification of furniture and the revival of interest in hand crafts, weaving and colouring with vegetable dyes; the interest in crewel work, which fitted into the interior schemes far better than needlepoint could do; and the decline in needlepoint itself seems natural. There was no longer a huge army of amateur embroiderers sitting at home with time on their hands. Professional embroiderers were there, as always, mending and restoring valuable pieces of embroidery, but for a long time amateur interest came and went fitfully. As far as needlepoint goes the most important outcome of the New Arts Movement was the establishing of embroidery schools, which evolved into, for example, the Royal School of Needlework. The existence of, among others, the Leek Society and the Ladies Work Society resulted in a new preoccupation with technical skill. Stitches were re-discovered and researched and studied, something that hadn't been done for a very long time. There are beautiful 'sampler' books from this time in the V & A containing enormous collections of stitches.

There is every reason to suppose that the age we live in will furnish us with more and more leisure time, and it is pretty certain that people will continue to place more and more value on hand-work that has involved imagination, labour and even human error. After a period of unpopularity canvas embroidery is indeed back in vogue. Ready-designed and coloured packs of canvas and wool are again produced in almost the same quantities as they were in the days of Berlin work. This time around the range is infinitely more varied and better. Nevertheless some are dull and coarse and others, while undeniably beautiful and desirable, are prohibitively expensive for the long-term embroiderer. Many of the good needlecraft shops are very generous with advice when customers turn to buying blank canvases and organising their own designs (shades of the Art Movement where the belief was that the best work was produced when designer and needleperson were one and the same).

The Schools of Needlework not only preserve the traditional, but experiment with new and abstract designs, often incorporating foreign elements: glass, metal, fabric, ribbon, beads. The successful results are truly spectacular (though you can imagine the mess when these disparate elements are not properly 'married').

In its time, canvas embroidery has been useful, purely decorative, utilitarian, nostalgic, genteel, snobbish, popular, élitist . . . It is no longer any one of those things and I suppose that all of us who are interested in it and enjoy doing it are in some way involved in the constant process of re-defining the nature of irrepressible needlepoint.

Basics

In the first place . . .

Should you grow to love needlepoint you will undoubtedly reach a stage where, let loose in a good shop, you will spend money like a drunken sailor. But all you actually need for the job is a piece of canvas, and a needle and yarn. However, mistakes are expensive and frustrating, so it's just as well to know something about your equipment: what sort of canvas is good for what sort of design and which yarn will give you the result you want. Now, you may very well start your canvas embroidery career as I did by buying a ready painted or drawn piece of canvas from a shop where an expert assistant will give you the appropriate yarn. (This is quite a good way of beginning as you stand an almost certain chance of producing something impressive on your first run-out and this gives a little courage to go on.)

Nevertheless, the moment will come when you will be stranded somewhere and unable to reach a shop, or you will be appalled at the amount of money you are getting through in your enthusiasm, or you will want to do something very personal and need to do your own design. It really is worth acquiring some technical knowledge. Processes that appear to be mysterious, arcane and impenetrable are very quickly mastered. I am what is loosely and inaccurately described as 'artistic' rather than 'practical'. I think it means that I used to have bright ideas and was too lazy to work them out. Learning to work them out was exhilarating and a lot simpler than I could have imagined.

Here's what you have to know about your equipment.

CANVAS

Needlework canvas is made of linen or cotton (usually cotton) or acrylic or plastic. Linen or cotton is long-lasting and pleasant to work with but there are instances where synthetics with their lack of 'give' might be appropriate (book covers, belts), though they would never be described as congenial to the fingers.

There are two main kinds of needlework canvas: *Mono* and *Penelope*.

Mono, which is usually offered in kits, is a canvas consisting of single threads evenly woven vertically and horizontally (the *warp* is vertical and the *woof* is horizontal).

Penelope canvas is double threaded. The vertical threads are closely twisted and the horizontal threads are spaced a little apart (the tightly-twisted threads should always run from the top to the bottom of your design).

The bulk of canvas sold in most shops nowadays is mono and although we have 'gone metric', people still calculate and buy by the inch. Stockists buy metric from abroad and then think and sell in imperial. Take your inch ruler and check the canvas for yourself in case your nearest stockist *is* thinking metric.

When you read about the 'size' of canvas, this refers to the size of the mesh, that is, how many threads there are to an inch (2.5 cm). Another word you might encounter is the 'gauge' of the canvas. This again is determined by the number of threads to an inch (2.5 cm). A 'Number 12 Mono' will have 12 threads to an inch vertically and horizontally (and so there are 144 stitches in a square inch (6.25 sq.cm) of 12 mesh Mono canvas).

Thirteen 'meshes' to an inch (2.5 cm) is a good general Mono canvas – it isn't so fine that it makes you feel like an old Turkish lacemaker, but it gives scope for considerable detail. Fine canvas goes from 18 to 40 mesh, coarse canvas suitable for a carpet can go from 5 to 14 mesh.

Penelope is a lovely, 'sympathetic' canvas. (People exaggerate the likelihood of confusion because of the double threads.) It is usually natural in colour and is very versatile. You can work the pairs of threads as though they are one, or you can split them and work double the stitches per inch. Say a Penelope canvas is ten squares to an inch (2.5 cm), it is referred to as 10/20 because you *can* work twenty squares to the inch (2.5 cm). You can see the advantage and convenience of this, I'm sure: while working a nice, fast, fairly 'gros' background, you can switch to a much finer stitch from a bit of pattern or detail within a pattern.

I usually work floor coverings in 8/16 Penelope and the work grows at a heartening speed. 10/20 is a good all purpose Penelope canvas.

Canvas comes in many widths. Fine mesh petit-point canvas is usually 24 inches (60 cm) wide. Other

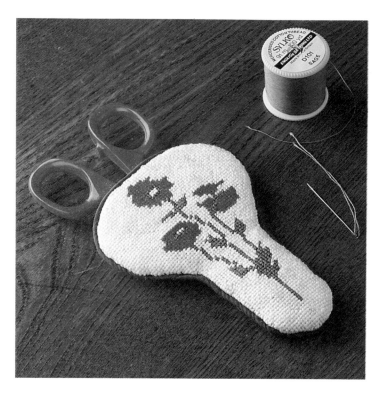

widths are 36 inches (90 cm) and 40 inches (100 cm). Buy canvas that is long enough. You can always cut off the spare bits and use them for small objects. (If you have a canvas that is much too big for your needs, cut it and 'bind' the edges in masking tape).

Check the canvas for defects or breaks or weaknesses. It will have to put up with a lot while you are working on it; animals love to curl up on unattended bits of embroidery; you might while travelling have to stuff it into your pocket; 'blocking' (*see page 108*) strains it even further and then it gets walked or sat on. Buy the best and strongest you can find.

NEEDLES

have to be blunt! Sharp needles hurt you (I have actually found traces of blood seeping on to a nice bit of petit-point which had to be unpicked – *see page 119*). They also hurt the work. The needle must pass easily through the hole without damaging or weakening the canvas, or causing the yarn to fray. If you have to force the needle into the hole, the needle is too big: if you have trouble dragging the needle out on the other side it is too small. Test the needle with the type of yarn you are going to be using because there is a double thickness of yarn at the eye and the needle must accommodate that extra bulk. A good 'average' size would be 18 or 19, though very fine needlepoint would call for something nearer 24 and a coarse

Flowers are a good source of 'round' designs. This one was copied from a Japanese textile design and is worked in stranded cotton on 20 mesh canvas using basketweave stitch for the front and straight Gobelin for the back.

It was made up using 8 inches of matching (though you could using contrasting) material, 4 inches of canvas or stiff fabric and a small square of felt.

canvas would take a 13. Make sure your needle is comfortable for you. Never use one that is rusty and have no compunction in throwing out a needle that doesn't feel 'right'.

YARN

In general natural fibres are much better than synthetic fibres. The colours are better, they last longer and they're nicer to work with. The finest, most versatile yarn of all is Persian yarn, which is 3-ply. The strands are loosely twisted (so they can be easily untwisted to one's pleasure). There are more than 400 colours available in this yarn and the effects are luxurious.

Tapestry yarn is 4-ply wool, generally available in traditional shades. (This is the original needlepoint yarn.) I use this doubled for 8/16 Penelope for floor coverings. A good firm will offer over 200 colours.

Crewel yarn is finer than tapestry or Persian yarn and it is lovely: strong, twisted 2-ply yarn, made from long fibrils of wool. The strands can be separated and one strand is perfect for fine work. Ravishing effects can be achieved by using combined strands of different shades or by shading from one tone into another. You can use multiple strands of crewel for coarser work. It lasts and lasts. Cotton or silk is suitable for fine work, but you have to bear with the fact that the strands tend to pull apart.

Knitting wools and crochet yarns are unsuitable; they fluff or stretch.

I have heard of but not yet encountered a French yarn called Bon Pasteur with an amazing range of colours which would be lovely for very detailed work.

Keep notes of how much yarn you use and you will soon become more expert than any shopkeeper at working out quantities. (There is nothing more maddening than running out of wool when you are not in a position to buy more.) When you are buying a lot of background wool try and get the sum right – or buy a bit more than is recommended; the dyes change slightly from batch to batch and you might not be able to match your wool.

The amount of wool used varies enormously according to the stitch used and also depends on the nature of the design and the fineness of the canvas. For example, 1 oz (28 gm) of wool will cover six square inches (37.5 sq. cm) of 14 mesh canvas sewn in tent stitch. Basketweave stitch will use up more wool on the same sized mesh, but the quantity of wool would be doubled if you wanted to cover a 6 mesh canvas properly.

Your other requirements are pretty ordinary; a nice, sharp little pair of scissors, a ruler, an indelible marker for the day when you begin to do your own designing, a frame should you wish (I have never used one as it makes work less portable but see page 102 for a simple design), a piece of fibre-board or cork and tin tacks for doing your own blocking.

Hand-work is what I call an 'instant heirloom'. Your work may well be in perfect condition a hundred years from now. It's worth investing in the best materials to hand.

Apart from canvas on display, the Women's Home Industries shop has lovely, rather battered folders full of well-thumbed drawings, sketches and photographs of designs, and pictures of upholstery and carpets and cushions worked by other clients. If a good idea presents itself to you and there's nothing like it in the shop, lurking in the background there's a very overworked artist who can commit it to paper or canvas, or tidy up your own amateur sketch. My mentor and task-master, Frankie Salter, has advised me and chivied me along and – not least – has prevented me from making bad and expensive choices of subject and material. The first rug I worked under her guidance was made up of squares with a large exotic tropical leaf on each and I sewed it in colours which I felt would fit in with the Connemara landscape for which it was intended.

The second rug was made from fifteen squares which I chose from among twenty-seven drawings based on details from the glorious 'Lady with the Unicorn' series of tapestries in the Cluny Museum in St Germain in Paris. The background colour in the original is red and pink and the ground colour at the base is red. I really needed dark blue and used that throughout as a background. This carpet lives in London and is constantly stamped on by all-comers and the cats. It is worked in double tapestry wool on 8 mesh Penelope canvas and is very tough.

The Essential Stitches

The basic needlepoint stitch is call *tent* stitch. The reason for its popularity is easy to perceive; it is good looking, durable and versatile, in fact it is the only stitch you *have* to learn. Also, joy of joys, it is just about the simplest stitch in existence, and although there are over a hundred variations, the basic form of the stitch is always the same. Any version of tent stitch covers the intersection of a vertical and horizontal thread (or in the case of Penelope canvas it covers the intersection of two pairs of threads). It is worked by introducing the needle from behind the canvas, bringing it through the hole on the bottom left of the intersection, drawing the wool diagonally upwards over the intersection and 'exiting' through the hole on the top right. Resist the temptation to vary this basic principle. It won't work. No matter how you are dodging around within your design maintain your bottom-left-diagonally-to-top-right movement. (If you have to turn your canvas, turn it 180° and continue your left-to-right stitch.)

The three most important versions of tent stitch are *half-cross*, *continental* and *basketweave*. It really is worth mastering these.

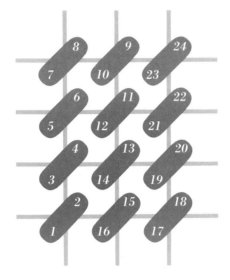 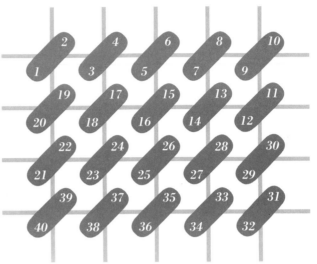

ABOVE LEFT: Upright half-cross (Tent)

ABOVE RIGHT: Half-cross (Tent)
Turn canvas 180° at end of row

Tent stitch in all its forms looks the same from the front, but looks completely different from the back and the versions vary in strength. The most economical but also the weakest is *half-cross* stitch. (Ideally, you should reserve this for use on Penelope canvas which helps to strengthen the stitch.) It is a useful stitch; as you see from the diagram you can travel horizontally or vertically and indeed you have to use it when fiddling around in small areas. Its disadvantage is that it tends to pull a big piece of canvas out of shape (but this can be remedied – see the section on blocking page 108), and because of its relative fragility it should be kept for things that are going to have an easy time of it (wall hangings, fire screens and so on). Turn the canvas 180° at the end of each row, which is worked from left to right.

The *continental* version of tent stitch uses up more wool but it is more hard-wearing. The stitch is exactly the same but it is worked from right to left all the way down the canvas. Again the canvas is turned 180° at the end of each row. Because it is stronger, this stitch is fine for objects that have to do a bit of living and

Continental (Tent)
Turn canvas 180° at end of row

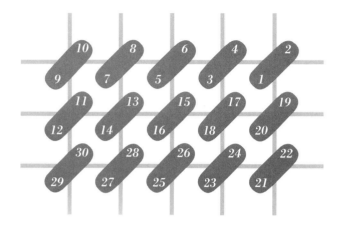

serves very well for cushions and upholstery. (Better behaved than half-cross, this also pulls out of shape but blocking is quite easy – *see page 108.*) Continental can be used on Penelope or Mono canvas.

Now we come to the major stitch in your needlepoint life: the *basketweave* tent. I cannot over-emphasise the importance of getting this one under your belt. It does everything anyone could ask of a stitch: it is

Basketweave (Tent)
Do not turn the canvas

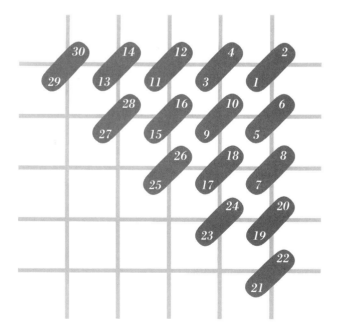

versatile and comfortable, you don't have to turn the canvas at the end of each row, it lasts and lasts and endures being walked on and messed about by children and animals; it is mendable, it doesn't distort and hardly needs any pulling back into shape; and it grows fast! Friends of mine who are much more skilful than I am but who started needlepointing by using half-cross stitch, claim that they cannot 'understand' basketweave. I am hopeless 'with my hands', as they say, but I think that basketweave is easy once you start thinking in diagonals instead of horizontals. Even if it's a *bit* confusing for the first half-hour, Low Cunning should keep the eye open to the fair advantage of comfort and speed, and that is usually enough to trigger off the will to win!

There is as much wool on the back of the canvas as there is on the front, hence the durability. When I am working a carpet in this stitch I gratefully remember Coral Browne's advice about not bothering to be too neat (neatness is not my strong point at the best of times so this was, rather, licence to kill). 'The more ends and "gunge" on the back, the nicer it is to walk on,' she said, looking improbably immaculate and, I suspect, incapable of doing anything 'gungy'. People pale when they see the backs of my carpets before they are mercifully covered over, but the fronts look all right and they *are* nice to walk on.

Now you know all you need to know in order to turn out some really smart needlepoint. You can go to the nearest good needlepoint store (thin on the ground) and buy yourself a ravishing, designed canvas, work it, take it back, have it done up and there you are with a lot of (earned) Brownie points and an instant heirloom. In the early stages this is a good idea but it is expensive. It's sensible to give yourself a present of a really well-designed canvas so that you have a beautiful kick-off and, frankly, after doing a lot of

At a party recently I found myself sitting next to theatrical producer Toby Rowlands and got to know Millie, his wife. Millie and I soon discovered that we had even more than we thought in common: needlepoint.

Her cushion is worked on quite a fine canvas, 14 mesh. Mrs Rowlands used five shadings of a colour in crewel wool. Crewel is made up of three strands which can be unravelled so that colours can be graded. You start each panel with three strands of the lightest shade and work that for a bit. Then drop one strand and adopt one from the next shade of the same colour. Next, drop another light strand and take up another darker one, so you are working with one strand of the original colour and two darker ones. Then move on to the darker shade entirely. Continue the process through all the shades to the centre. Millie's cushion is worked in five panels, using the palest colour as the background for the centre panel. Work the design on this panel, and, if you use beads as Millie has done, her advice is to stretch the embroidered canvas before applying the beads.

hard work on something it is worth getting it professionally finished so that the labour is properly presented. However, and it is a big however and a big stride into the mysteries of the Back Room, it is worth learning all the processes because there is nothing quite as much fun as regarding one's own, specially designed, drawn up, sewn, pressed, finished 'object'. (By this time it attains the prestige of an 'objet'.)

I hope during the following chapters to show you how all this is attainable. Many of you will be naturally gifted with needle and yarn. I am not, so the pace might prove a trifle slow from time to time. (I have to reproduce my own solutions to the problems that I, as a novice, encountered and some of you will wish to skip some of the really obvious sections.) To those of you who, like me, are not at all sure if they can do anything, stay with me. If I can do this, anyone can.

ADDITIONAL STITCHES

Although the basic stitches equip you to do anything you wish, there will probably come a moment when you will feel like enlarging your technique, and I've chosen some dozen or so 'extra' stitches which will give you spectacular results without too much brain damage. (Actually, I would suggest that if you are starting needlepoint, or if you are interested in design only, you should skip this section till you can look at it later, at leisure.)

The upright version of tent stitch is *Gobelin* stitch. This is worked left to right or right to left in horizontal rows. The yarn covers from two to six threads. (I've shown it over two threads.) Come in at 1, cross the two threads vertically and 'exit' at 2, come down at the back and through at 3, and so on. You are always working from the bottom to the top of the stitch. If you are working over more than two threads, you have to watch out for pulling and snagging. Be very careful to make a full, relaxed stitch. (If you pull you will expose canvas.) This stitch is very good for edgings, and you see it as background in very early needlework.

Slanted Gobelin You merely lean the same stitch over, one thread to the right. Come in at 1 and draw the

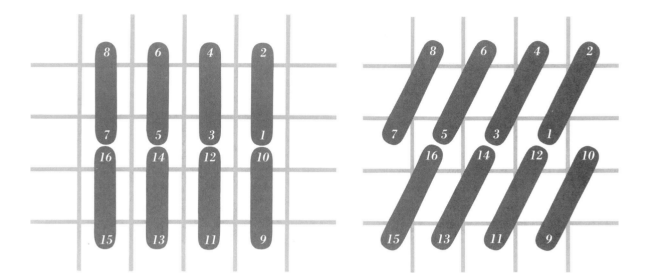

ABOVE LEFT: Straight Gobelin

ABOVE RIGHT: Slanted Gobelin

thread up and to the right, and 'exit' at 2. (This can be worked over more threads.) Actually, this is often used to imitate 'old' tapestry, and you'll see why if you work an inch or two.

Encroaching Gobelin As you see from the diagram, this is simply slanted Gobelin with the next row down pushed up into the one above. Work right to left, then return to the right and fit your stitch into the one above so you achieve a very close texture.

Encroaching Gobelin

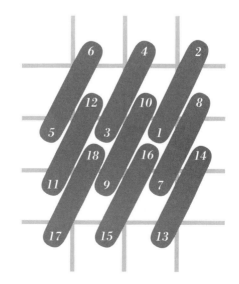

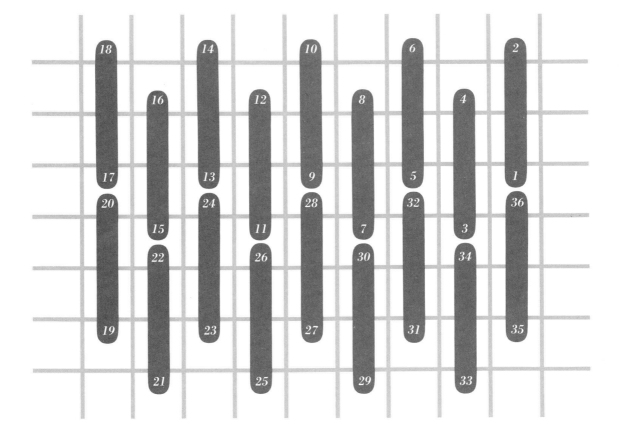

Brick

Brick stitch is the stitch that is used for Bargello (*see page 49*). It is also a derivation of the upright Gobelin. Some people insist this should be worked from left to right, but I have always done it from right or left (and that is how I've shown the diagram). The stitch looks best covering three or four threads. If you are working four threads, drop down two threads for the next stitch, and if you are working only three drop down one. This 'drop' formation resembles a brick wall. There will be end bits, top and bottom, which you have to fill in with little upright stitches.

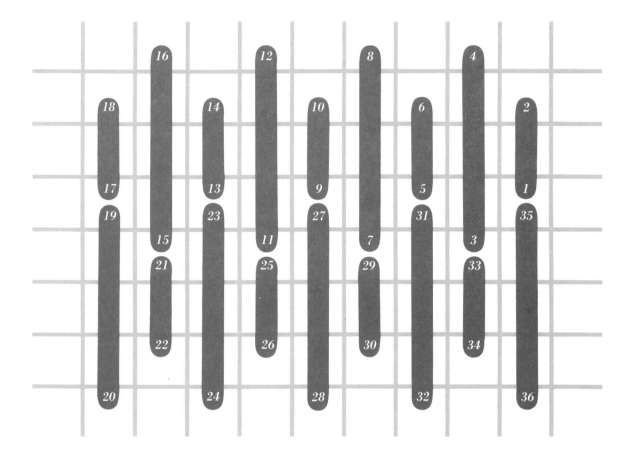

Parisian

Parisian stitch looks like brick stitch. The difference is that you work one long and one short stitch alternately. The long stitches are worked over three or four threads, and the short ones cover one or two threads. The canvas is turned completely at the end of each row, and the colours can only be changed from row to row.

Mosaic stitch is one of the best of all background stitches; it is interesting and gives a nice texture without being obtrusive and busy. It consists of

43

Mosaic

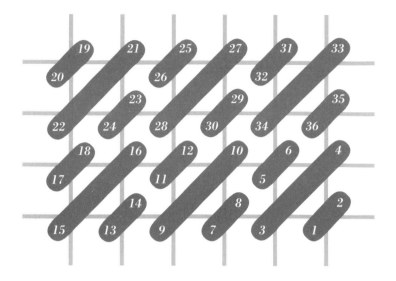

diagonal stitches all going in the same direction and three stitches (one long, flanked by two short) make up a small square. It can be worked diagonally, in which case there is no need to turn the canvas. I usually work it from right to left, turning the canvas 180° at the end of each row, and that is how I've arranged the diagram.

Cashmere stitch is another beautiful background and border stitch. It differs from mosaic stitch in that you use two long stitches at the centre of each group. Complete a group before moving on to the next. You can work from right to left or left to right or diagonally – whichever way you find comfortable. I've drawn it worked from right to left. When you have completed a whole row, turn the canvas 180° and work the second row in precisely the same way.

You can play around almost indefinitely with the slanting stitch used for mosaic and cashmere. If you work a square of diagonals you get *Scottish* stitch. This is a good, fast-growing background. If you then add an outline of half-cross stitches around each square, it gives a really interesting plaid effect. (There is no need to turn the canvas at the end of each row.)

Cashmere

RIGHT: Scottish
(Next row worked right to left)

BELOW: Scottish with border
(Next row worked right to left)

Byzantine

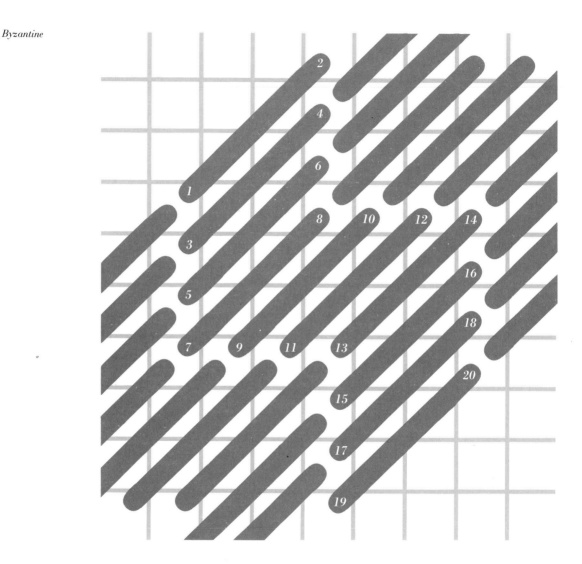

Byzantine stitch is another excellent, interesting background stitch. This is usually worked in groups of four slanting stitches, each of which covers three threads. Once you have worked one zig-zag row, it is extremely easy to continue and it grows fast. The yarn is brought in at the lower left hand point of the stitch and then taken three threads across and three up to the right. (Should you wish you could vary this and work over four threads arranging your stitches in groups of six.)

Cross Stitch

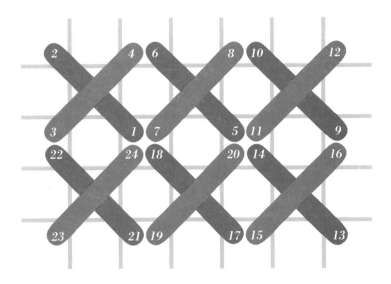

With *cross* stitch we come to a very important group of stitches. Basic cross stitch is a development of tent· stitch made by working across two threads of the canvas from bottom right to top left and then from bottom left to top right to complete one stitch. Move horizontally from left to right and from right to left. It is better to complete each cross before moving to the next. This method gives a very firm, well-covered, strong finish.

The *Greek cross* is very stable and quick to work. Each stitch must be completed before you move to the next. Work from left to right and turn the canvas

Greek Cross Stitch

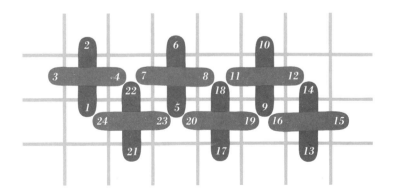

Leviathan (Smyrna) Cross

180° at the end of each row (so you always move from left to right).

The *Leviathan* (or *Smyrna*) *cross* takes longer. Each cross must be completed before you go on to the next. Work from left to right and work the next row from right to left without turning the canvas.

Rice is a very smart stitch. You begin by making a large cross stitch (say, over four threads). Then make diagonal stitches over the corners of each cross moving in an anti-clockwise direction. Try the large cross in a different colour from the little surface stitches. Work the big crosses from right to left, then 'complete', adding the little stitches, moving from left to right. Then, without turning the canvas, start your second row in the same way as the first.

Bargello deserves a book to itself. The variations are endless, but the method is very easy. All you are dealing with is a series of upright stitches worked in repeat patterns. Don't be confused by the names: Hungary point, Florentine, flame stitch. It seems that

Rice

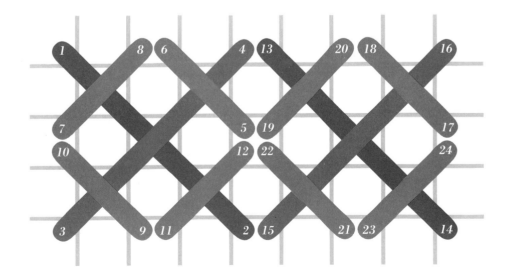

When I was filming with Robert Hardy and feeling a bit blue because I'd been obliged to start wearing glasses, 'Tim's' secretary and general factotum, Wendy Garcin, made me a consolatory specs case. It's the only one I've never lost, though I've lost at least ten pairs of glasses. It's Bargello, lined with velvet.

BELOW AND OPPOSITE: Various forms of Bargello

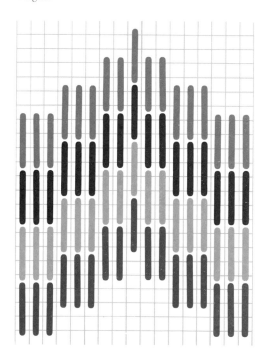

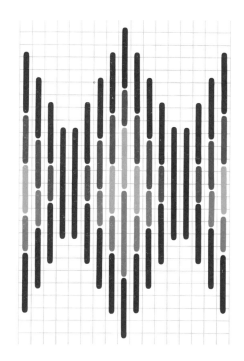

the stitch was introduced to Italy from Hungary, and Bargello is actually the name of a museum in Florence which contains very fine examples of chairs upholstered in Florentine canvas work. (Because the yarn doesn't cross canvas intersections, there is no chance of the work pulling out of shape so it never needs to be blocked, and this saves lots of time.) Once

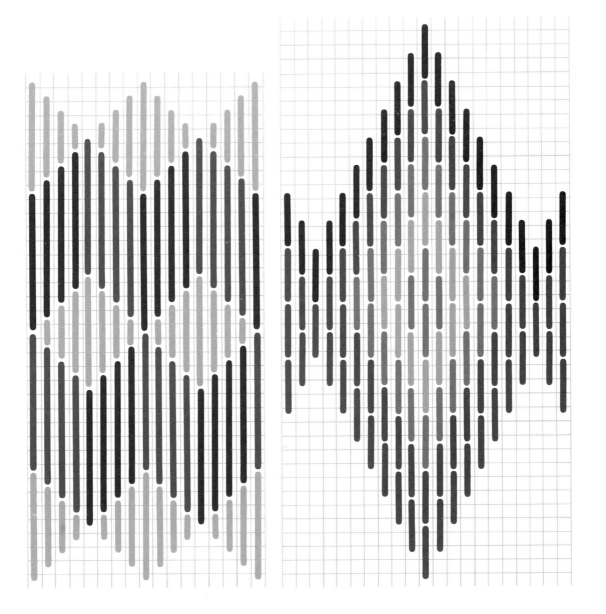

you have worked one line choosing your dips and curves and peaks, it is wonderfully easy to copy the row immediately below. Traditionally the stitchery is worked in many shades of one colour. I was quite bowled over when I started 'doodling' one day and realised that, for all its imperfections, my free-hand canvas was really very good-looking. It is also a lovely way of using up left-over wool; one can introduce 'shock' colours, and invariably one's improvisations look as though they were intended. I've shown one or two 'classic' designs, and a few 'doodles' which you can improve on indefinitely.

There are so many more stitches . . . There are useful little handbooks describing over a hundred, and once you have worked your way through the basic tent (and maybe a few fancier ones) you will find the instructions perfectly easy to interpret. I realise now that it would have saved me endless trouble as a beginner had I worked a sampler of four or five stitches just for my own confidence (and it would have been a good souvenir). Rather late in the day I have made one up (*see page 59*) and I suggest that you buy a bit of Mono canvas and some Anchor wools and make up your own. If it's a disaster, it doesn't matter; it won't have cost you much and you can keep the canvas for practice. If it's half-way decent, you may find that you have a very pretty little 'primitive' picture that you'll be happy to keep and frame.

LEFT HANDED NEEDLEPOINT

I unwittingly did something awful to my Aunt Toffee.
Not unusually, having bitten off more than I could
chew and with major disasters looming on several
fronts, artistic and domestic, I rounded up what
family I could find (daughter Pat, who had a bit of
time off from her drama school, my truly belle-mère,
Eleanor Summerfield, who is a marvellous seamstress
and knitter and who wasn't too pressed in her
comedy play, and Toffee, also a brilliant knitter and
designer of knitwear, who was between projects), and
having assembled them I delivered a short talk on
needlepoint, demonstrated basketweave and exited
hurriedly leaving them with half an acre of
background work. I thought Toffee looked a bit
bemused . . . She completed her assignment all right
but it nearly drove her mad. I had completely
forgotten that she was left-handed! Being
conscientious she had somehow managed to follow
my right-handed instructions, but of course left-
handers should work their stitches in a different
direction. There is however no need to resort to
turning instructions upside-down or holding the
instructions up to the mirror.

Left-Handed Half-Cross Stitch

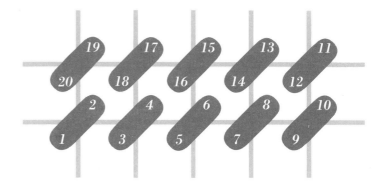

This is the left-handed diagram for half-cross stitch.

Come through to the front on the odd numbers and complete the stitch, going through to the back on the even numbers. Turn the canvas 180° at the end of each row.

Left-Handed Continental Stitch

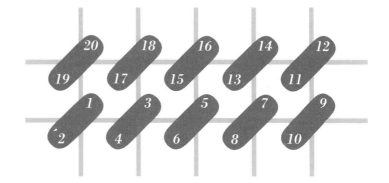

Continental stitch for left-handers

Work from left to right, stitches pointing down, and turn the canvas completely at the end of each row.

Basketweave stitch begins in the bottom left-hand corner of the canvas and the first stitch points down, not up.

Left-Handed Basketweave

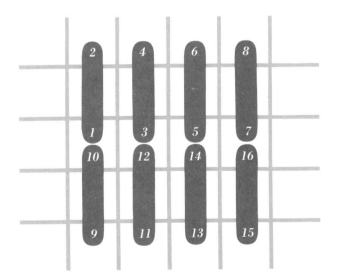

Here are some diagrams for a few more stitches.

Left-Handed Straight Gobelin Stitch

Left-handed Slanting Gobelin Stitch

Left-Handed Cross-Stitch
Complete each cross before going on to the next

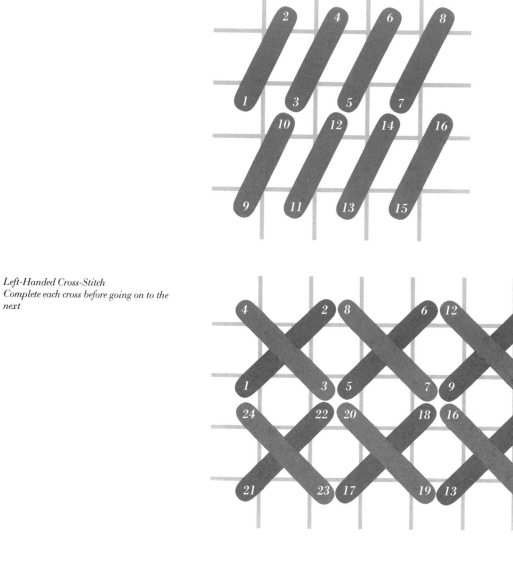

Don't forget that, direction apart, the rules that apply to right-handers also apply to you!

SAMPLERS

Trying to analyse my great fondness for samplers I finally decided that it must arise from their combination of intrinsic beauty and their very personal link with the past. They are undeniably attractive; the most complex being beautifully skilled and the simplest so touching in their evidence of hard work and the *lack* of skill which becomes an extra attraction. To do a spelling sampler and to spell a word wrong is endearing; to misjudge the number of threads and to have to chop up a word must have been shaming for the small seamstress but it raises a very sympathetic smile from us some hundred years later.

Strictly speaking samplers ought not to be in this book. They were not generally worked on 'canvas' as we know it but sewn on linen or cotton and are really counted-thread embroidery. The majority we encounter were worked in cross stitch. But they do have the 'feel' of needlepoint and originated as needlepoint 'text-books'. Though I would like to try a traditional sampler on linen, I intend for a while to pursue the possibilities of working samplers on open canvas. My first attempt is not pleasing me very much; I've put in an accurate picture of our house and added 'emblems': our three cats, some of the pigs

This is the sampler which I finished off mainly out of stubbornness: I am not at all happy with it and plan a better one. I think that my 12 mesh canvas simply was not fine enough for my purpose. (I used two strands of Persian yarn.)

This stitch sampler is worked on 16 mesh canvas. This is my favourite size for upholstery or any Bargello work. Many of the squares are worked in two strands of Persian yarn and others were done in left-over bits of tapestry wool. There are no prizes for guessing which square was sewn in British Rail light on a train from Norwich. (It will be corrected – later . . .)

which I collect, our initials, the date when we moved in. There are some border patterns taken from eighteenth century American quilts and a tree of life (on which my birds look like fishes), and there's a dove of peace in a tree which looks a bit like a cross vulture with a bit of broccoli in its mouth. There are also some 'sample' stitches and there is, I think, too much, in the wrong way. A more traditional approach will be heaps more effective, but it's worth persevering with this 'personal' sort of sampler, because after all the original purpose of the sampler is long gone. Its development is fascinating, however, and gives some inkling of what the future might hold.

Originally, as you might imagine, a sampler was an 'example'. It was a kind of reference book in the form of a long, narrow piece of fabric on which were sewn bands of stitches, and there are references to such samplers from the early sixteenth century. From the time of the advent of printed pattern books the basic necessity of the sampler was gone, but books were not then generally available, nor were they for a very long time. (Not surprising when you consider that, once again in the 1980's, we are short of school textbooks.) I imagine that the early samplers were rolled up and kept in the work box much in the way that one keeps one's booklet of illustrated stitches in one's sewing bag. When 'my beste sampler' is left to a daughter in her mother's sixteenth century will, one can be pretty sure that it was not intended to be a purely decorative bequest.

Gradually, the actual shape of samplers changed, growing shorter and wider over the years and becoming more like a decorative picture, incorporating little figures, and flowers, then letters and houses and beasts and numbers.

Until the eighteenth century, almost forty stitches
could be seen demonstrated (the most favoured
stitches seeming to be Roumanian, Rococo cross,
long-armed cross, plaited braid and montenegrin).
By the next century some twenty stitches had
disappeared, while the subject matter became even
more informal and pictorial in character. Little scenes
occupied the centre of the picture and the bands of
stitches which used to occupy the entire sampler have
moved out to the sides and into the borders.

Of course the sampler had a continuous use as a
medium for the teaching of children. There are –
what we now consider to be – beautiful 'darning'
samplers and these would have been laboured over by
little girls whose lives might well have depended on
their skill with a needle. The plain 'band' samplers
which have a special, austere appeal would have been
worked by children learning button-holing, mending,
renovating, 'turning' – all the techniques necessary
for maintaining the personal and household linen
belonging to their employers in the days before sewing
machines.

Less affecting are the writing and geography samplers
worked by children who were at school and not
necessarily destined for 'service'. It's not totally clear
to me that sewing a map of England is the most
efficient way of learning its counties and principal
towns, but one's sewing would undoubtedly improve
and the results are eminently desirable and
collectable. As for the writing samplers, my favourites
are the ones that go a bit wrong, with some letters
sewn backwards and not quite enough room allowed
for all of them.

Mottoes and quotations from the Bible (all
depressing) occupied the energy of the nineteenth
century sampler worker. Mercifully, human nature

Even as a little girl my grandmother was not given to making mistakes, and this is a very respectable rendering of our very Welsh family home on the Bettws mountain. We're very grateful for it because, strangely, there are no photographs and since it was sold the trees are gone, the garden and farm buildings destroyed, and this farm, orderly as the sampler, built by my great-grandmother, and where my grandmother, my mother and I were born, is quite lost. (Permission of Mrs Meriel Lewis; photograph by Arwel Davies)

being what it is, the average child was extremely unlikely to have been cast down by the miserable sentiments she was obliged to commit to posterity (at eight, one just doesn't *believe* that life is short and nasty). There is a uniformity about Victorian samplers which, if they are considered en masse, makes them seem a bit dull, but they're so hard to come by nowadays that I never have enough to get tired of them, and I take a good deal of pleasure in imagining a really *wicked* girl fairly absent-mindedly and only half-mutinously sewing

This is a very fine 'homestead' sampler, worked by my cousin, Jenny Lewis, in silk on a ground of 28 mesh. She has shown her childhood home and all the trees and plants are chosen from among those that are indigenous to the neighbourhood. (The elms, of course, are no more.) Having first worked out the design on graph paper, Jenny used tent stitch, encroaching Gobelin (for the fields), brick stitch (for the walls and trees) with some French knots as well. She admits that it was a trifle hard on the eyes! (Permission of Mrs Gethin Lewis, photograph by Arwel Davies)

The very first decorative object that Robin and I were given when we were setting up house (and getting very bored with having to limit our shopping to hardware stores and washing-machine shops) was a lovely little eighteenth century blue and white sampler, the gift of actress and art expert, Adrienne Corri. It was an inspired shot-in-the-dark present and is the basis of my sampler collection. Even Ada (who is a sort of white witch) could hardly have envisaged where her present would lead me . . .

This one has a charming 'mistake' in spacing and the lay-out makes the message fairly inaccessible at first sight.

'The fairest Virgin in the world
Must in the dust be laid.'

Challenged she would probably reject all that dust as
having nothing to do with her in much the same way
as my great-grandmother, unable to avoid noticing
that she came from a long line of tough long-living
Welsh peasants (she lived to a normal 96) and feeling
full of life, would have had to admit that she thought
that her message about man being here today and
gone tomorrow and sunk without a trace was
probably meant to apply to those Lewises in the next
valley. One is free to enjoy these samplers without
suffering misplaced feelings of sadness at the lot of the
depressed seamstresses.

All this time, girls who *were* going to lead depressed
lives were still working away at the (I think) more
distinguished, plain samplers. (I wonder were they
ever used as audition pieces by talented girls who
ambitiously wanted a position in a really great
household? Mending the Queen's lace nightie must
have seemed a really super job.)

The advent of the sewing machine made countless
thousands of women redundant, and although fine
work is, to this day, best hand done, the mending of
everyday things was turned over to the machine and
the making of all except haute couture clothes was no
longer the province of the mistress of stitchery.
Samplers as *aide-memoires* were completely
redundant; girls began to be properly educated; they
needed to solve problems, not merely know 'figures';
'letters' were something to write home with, not sew,
and learning to work machines, drive cars, turn out
munitions and take deep breaths before pole-vaulting
into the centre stage of politics and finance and
industry meant that they just didn't have the idle

hands which previously had needed to be occupied lest the devil should move in, providing them with something really fascinating to do.

As it has turned out, this removal of the amateur hand has been a good thing. Samplers are a part of history and we can collect them, treasure them, copy them, or invent bits and pieces of amusing contemporary samplers, but work of this kind which does not have a root in useful life cannot maintain a convincing presence. Fortunately what has happened is that the professionals have made a welcome return; early in this century, as a result of the work being done in the schools of art, a record was made of scores of 'lost' stitches. (Miss Louisa Pesel's stitch samplers were made for and are still housed at the Victoria & Albert Museum.) After the Second World War much ecclesiastical needlepoint needed to be replaced and samplers were professionally made and sent out into the country and provinces where work of first-class standard was undertaken by previously inexperienced needleworkers. It is gladdening to see the revival of the teaching sampler.

In present day 'amateur' samplers the motto and the alphabet are out of fashion, but people do like portraying their houses and gardens and for examples of those one can look to the past for help and inspiration. Stitch samplers are becoming popular, not for teaching but for their decorative effect. Cross stitch, which became the supreme sampler stitch in the nineteenth century, is now used in conjunction with traditional stitches from earlier periods, and these stitches are of prime importance in the appearance and interest of the contemporary sampler. It is too convenient and attractive a concept to disappear. It remains to be seen what its next mutation will be.

PROJECTS AND SOURCES OF IDEAS

Canvas embroidery is at its most personal when it has been made for giving away. The time spent planning and making something for a friend's birthday or to commemorate a special occasion seems to pass much more quickly than the time spent in making one's own piano-stool seat. The anticipation of the delight you will witness when your gift is unwrapped (and the prospect of the astonished praise and love coming your way) increases the harder you work. So the needle simply flies . . . It is not surprising then that, in time, most of us acquire a glory hole stuffed with half-finished canvases, drawings, notes for canvases as yet unborn, all of them laid aside in favour of something irresistibly asking to be made for someone *else* (and the bags of yarn . . . sometimes I stand for a long time wondering why there seems to be about a mile of *cerise*, for heaven's sake!).

So from time to time I make a clean sweep of my unfinished projects. Once the torture of opening a show called *Pal Joey* was over and I had more or less regained my senses and was safely tucked into a nice big dressing-room in St Martin's Lane, I forced myself to *finish* everything that had been started. Almost the nicest part of a long-running show is the backstage life. (In fact, at times there's more going on

We have three Burmese cats and when I was given a painted canvas of a Siamese I altered it a bit to look like Spencer, my Burmese blue, and feel gratified when he leans on it. He's worked in continental stitch.

67

backstage than on-stage and sometimes it's a lot more interesting.) But during *Pal Joey* when I wasn't singing I was *sewing*. Heavens, some of it was boring but after a year I was 'up' four cushions and a foot-stool, the glory hole was bare — and I had acquired a new lot of projects . . .

Not for the first time I'd been dressed for this show by John Bates. Whenever a stage direction says anything remotely like 'Enter centre stage looking wonderful' my shaking hand flies to the phone to ask the management to summon the cavalry in the shape of J.B., whose clothes and moral support have got me through many a sticky moment in life as well as in the theatre. He recently gave me a present which has sparked off a few new ideas. I do 'initial' cushions all the time (there's one for Robin on the couch pictured on page 115). If you acquire an alphabet book nothing could be easier than to enlarge your chosen letter and then add a bit of greenery or a trailing flower. Now I have a new method based on the hand-embroidered ribbons that John Bates gave me. Instead of doing a plain letter and decorating around it, I plan to draw a large Roman capital with a plain background and fill the letter itself with flowers copied from the ribbons. On a less sophisticated level it would be fun to fill the letter with lots and lots of little primitive designs, like the fragments of embroidery based on the work of the Mexican artist the late Manuel Lépé (who always drew and painted little angel children and trees of life and amusing birds and bees). The shirt on to which these were appliquéd disintegrated with age but I've cut off the embroidery which has survived beautifully. John Bates' ribbons are also going to be used as 'mats' inside picture frames and it might be interesting at some point to needlepoint mats in the Victorian manner. (John Bates' ribbons are illustrated on page 70, and Manuel Lépé's designs on page 71.)

To my chagrin I realise that none of my ideas is absolutely original. In fact, in my experience, the best methods for acquiring good ideas can be summed up in one word – *theft*. There are two actresses who drive me to the extremes of larceny and they are both American – Mary Martin and Sylvia Sidney.

I recently worked for director John Irman and not only was he very understanding about my sewing-to-a-deadline-while-acting, but he magically summoned out of the air from America a book which is unobtainable here. It is by Sylvia Sidney whom I knew only as a movie star but she is also a wonderful embroiderer (and a breeder of pugs. In fact the fruits of these combined activities can be seen in the photographs of the Duchess of Windsor's French sitting-room. Look out for Sylvia Sidney's

Manuel Lépé's designs

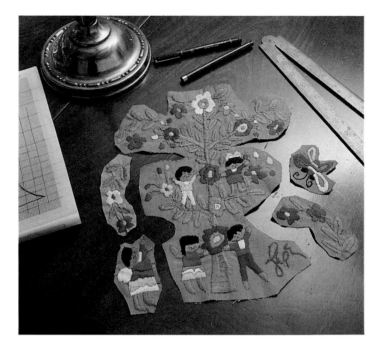

needlepoint cushions of the pugs, beloved of the Duchess as well). All the embroidery in *her* book is from original designs (and nearly all presents for other people!). One of the most beautiful is a small 'ring cushion' for a wedding ceremony. It's worked on very fine canvas and shows 'antique-style' true lovers' knots top and bottom with the combined Christian-name initials at the centre where the gold bands would rest. Another of her cushions has a very pretty geometric border and only gradually does one realise that the pattern is the repeat of a monogram.

This can be applied to an entire cushion, and I'm told that Judi Dench employs this method to devastating effect. (It is extraordinary the things one doesn't know about people; I had no idea till recently that Judi was an avid embroiderer.) It seems that she's been known to make consoling presents for colleagues who have been set upon by less than kind directors and her short, sharp comment on the offending

John Bates' ribbons

'gauleiter' is joined up into a repeat pattern so that the casual observer might never realise that there was a message in the medium.

Mary Martin's book has been a treasure-trove since I borrowed it many years ago. Sadly, it also is out of print and unavailable here so I had to depend on the good offices of a mutual friend, Stanley Hall (who benevolently dominated the theatrical wig and make-up party scene here for more years than he'd care me to mention), who came through with a copy of my very own. I keep drawing and re-drawing my version of a 'souvenir' rug (a straight 'steal'). Miss Martin's is exquisite – pale background, little dividing ribbons of ivy and small motifs of things that are important in her life: small picture of a house, initials of children, favourite flowers, significant dates. It looks a bit like this.

And if you couldn't bear to walk on it, it would look lovely as a wall hanging.

Noel Coward called it 'That Damn' Carpet'. It weighed a ton and she carried it around the world, finally working on it backstage during the long run of *The Pajama Game* (with her son Larry Hagman in the chorus). She managed to finish it just before Princess Margaret was due to visit the theatre. Noel Coward, escorting, opened the dressing-room door to reveal a beaming Miss Martin who had just that second flung down 'That Damn' Carpet', and he raised his eyes to heaven in gratitude that it was all over as The Royal Foot descended.

Miss Martin has also brilliantly solved the problem of 'portrait' needlepoint. I had always assumed that it was futile to attempt to sew likenesses of people (the faces always look like puddings), but had made a mental note that silhouette portraits might work very well indeed. I didn't take the idea further, but Mary Martin capitalised on the fact that you don't need features to render a likeness, and when she made a cushion for Oscar Hammerstein she showed him, composing, in a characteristic reclining position, and virtually omitted the head except for a vague outline. Going even further, her cushion of Richard Rodgers shows his hands at his desk, composing *Bali Hai*. One can see the jacket, tie and shirt, the hands, wrist watch, table and manuscript and nothing else, and it's quite unmistakably Richard Rodgers.

Neither Miss Sidney nor Miss Martin ever had a needlework lesson, and it is very encouraging to think that they were able to struggle through by trial and error to arrive at outstandingly successful solutions to very difficult problems of taste and technique.

This is a coffee table with embroidery under the glass, owned by Shana Alexander. The turtle design and the canvas is from 'Alice Maynard' on Madison Avenue, New York. Among other things, Shana is the author of six books, an 'international brain' on Radio 4, an award-winning journalist, a radio and TV personality and the founder of the National Women's Political Caucus of America. And she still finds time for needlepoint . . . (Photo by Shana Alexander)

All my finished brick door-stops have been given away. My current brick (for a 'star' of my acquaintance and not theatrical!) is drawn and cut out. The cutout canvas is shown overleaf. The better drawn butterfly brick in the photograph is the work of a WHI artist. When you have finished embroidering, sew up with wrong sides together, leaving room for the brick to be inserted. Iron the turnings flat, turn right side out and finish sewing up.

The brick is not my idea either, it is a WHI notion and I cannot imagine why I have left it unfinished since I desperately need it. Some of our doors close themselves, unbidden, and if the cats are denied entry (or egress) they fly into a rage and take up the carpets round the doors (so they *have* to be propped open). These are very good presents and all mine have been given away, so I'll show two canvases; one is beautifully drawn up by the artist-in-residence at the WHI and the other is rather badly 'indicated' by me but it'll look just fine when it's sewn because I have by me a book given to me by Lynda La Plante which shows needlepoint based on Italian mosaics, and the star design is lovely in the original which I shall more or less copy. The diagram overleaf shows how the canvas should be cut to fit a standard UK brick.

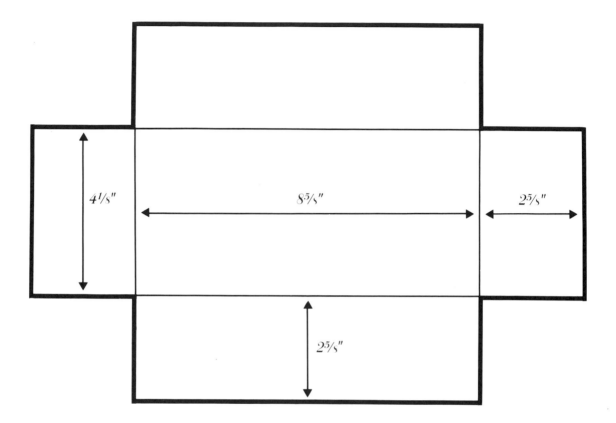

The whole thing is assembled in the same way as one would sew a hassock.

Lynda, whom I met at dawn in a windowless vintage car stationary in a field in the driving rain in Kent (such are the joys of filming) when she was planning her successful TV series *The Widows*, typically took an avid interest in the damp bit of canvas I was 'getting on with' and she gave me a piece of needlepoint which she'd found in the attic of a house she'd bought. It was black, and she bravely washed it. (It looks 1930s to me and it's worked entirely in rice stitch.) I didn't want to make it into a cushion, nor did I want to frame it and the other day I saw a solution in the shape of useful *little* occasional tables made of framed, glassed over pieces of needlework or textiles, placed on extra-short stubby legs (like three large cotton reels placed one on top of the other and painted). No-one ever has enough flat surfaces for people to put things on and it's nice to have something interesting to look at when you pick up an olive.

Wallpaper is a good general source of ideas. The difficulty with repeat patterns is that one doesn't know how well one will like a design when it is repeated many times. Well, wallpaper shows you exactly what a repeat looks like. Textiles are an equally fruitful source. In fact look around for things that are already 'placed' in their space since this is, I find, one of the chief headaches when designing: putting things in the right place in space. Old plates are wonderfully helpful. I collect those rather silly 'Present from . . .' plates and the little fruits or flowers or views are beautifully positioned in the circle. Very often one doesn't even have to alter the scale. If one had a whole series of grand dessert plates one could make a lovely carpet quite easily ('my Spode carpet in the study . . .').

Finding a series of things – like the dessert plates – is very helpful. I borrowed a book of Chinese characters and traced six that had a pretty shape and generally applicable translations ('strength' and 'prosperity' and so on). One is completed, and Robin took it to a Chinese supermarket to ensure that in scaling it up I hadn't changed the meaning. (Awful if 'Peace and Prosperity' became in my ignorant hands 'Residents Parking Only'.) Apparently it is all right and I shall go on to do another five using the same colours but changing the background stitch in each. My mother-in-law (who has leapt from beginner status to expert in six months) will be in charge of the textured backgrounds.

Penelope Keith's cushion.

One of my projects that took far too long to complete is Beryl Reid's cat. (It is photographed being stretched – *see page 107* – so any minute now it will be in Honey Pot Cottage being sat on by one of eleven cats-in-residence.) Of course, my Miss Reid has come up with a much better idea: the whole square blank (acres of background sewing) and in the bottom right-hand corner the tip of the tail of a disappearing cat. I wish I'd thought of that.

It must be apparent that I am an animal-lover and I have to restrain myself from running riot with animal needlepoint because I am aware that too much in the way of lovesome beasts can prove very resistible to many people. Not surprisingly, a notable exception is Penny Keith's dog-cushion. She always has corgis and this dear-departed one's initial is shown on a cushion which is filled with his (washed) hair-combings. 'When the others misbehave,' she said, '*I point at the cushion.*' I wonder if they roll over and laugh or do they absorb this stern reminder of mortality?

This is March and I've just finished a Christmas project. I have about six to go and this year I *will*

Mair's boot.

finish them all. Some years ago I spent Christmas with my friends the Brunings in Venice, and Leslie who is a good needlewoman made red Christmas 'boots' for me and my two daughters. This moved me to consider needlepoint boots for all my nephews and nieces in Wales. ('Consider' is almost all I've done so far. Mair's is finished.) Each one will incorporate the name or initial and a general festooning with balloons, stars, holly and Santas worked mainly in red and green and white and they should be nice things to keep from year to year. Very little boots make pretty Christmas tree decorations (and grown-ups might even find small bottles of scent or little jewels inside – or a truffle would do, I suppose).

On a rather larger scale I have under way a bed project, and the design of the appliquéd panels is copied from a wallpaper border book which I found in the V & A museum shop. (The centre panel which is as yet not committed to canvas, will be based on flowers, cut in stone.) My original colours had to be abandoned as the Burmese cats have only a short run in winter from mud, via cat-door, to bed. So pastels are out and the colour scheme will be on the sombre side. Once the spread is completed, I can see that druggets and an end-of-the-bed stool will demand to be sewn and there will be a reproachful mound of unfinished canvases in the corner of the room for some time to come.

Ideas . . . there are too many for comfort. 'Star-signs' . . . everyone, even the unbeliever, seems to like the Zodiac signs and every magazine has ready-made drawings to choose from.

The kitchen and garden provide an endless supply of designs – seed-pods, dissected cabbages, green peppers, seed-heads, magnolia grandiflora leaves: shiny green above, felted rust underneath.

There is one notion I keep being given and which I have not got around to trying (but it seems so good that I pass it on, just as an idea). Stained glass . . . already cut up and very simple in outline. Until recently I didn't try it because, to me, stained glass meant dark, jewel-coloured, ecclesiastical glass and I really couldn't envisage being able to accommodate that at home. Then I went to work at the George Lucas studio and ranch in northern California. Mr Lucas is by way of being a sort of latter day Renaissance patron of the arts. Craftsmen and artists and writers and inventors live in the most idyllic surroundings doing whatever it is they feel they do best and the visitor can see the incidental results all around, in the small model villages that also house the staff 'canteen' where the floors and doors and window frames are made of beautiful wood; the lamps and door furniture are made by first-rate craftsmen; the pastry chef has just defected from the best restaurant in San Francisco; and the stained glass is so beautiful that one would like to wrap it up and take it home. The Lucas glass workers have beaten the Tiffany Company many times to become the national prize winners in stained glass and it is a revelation: pale, pale colours and exquisite secular representations of flowers and beasts and birds. These are things one could very profitably copy. We have no examples here, alas, but, my eyes having been opened in the United States, I have realised that William Morris stained glass (at least, the examples I have seen in private houses in London) is very 'modern' and very like contemporary American glass. I feel sure that this is an avenue well worth exploring.

I suppose this is the charm of needlepoint – it enables all of us to become 'artists' of a sort if only for a moment; it provides endless avenues to explore, and best of all one never 'arrives'. It is, like gardening or acting, an occupation with, thank goodness, no end in sight . . .

Your Own Canvas Start To Finish

It seems a far cry from buying a kit to designing one's own canvas (well, it *is* quite a step), but if you feel inclined to give it a try, you will find yourself on a very exciting, if occasionally nerve-racking, road.

Once you start working out projects and suiting your embroidery to your own taste and to your home, your friends, your occupation and your family, you will open a floodgate of ideas. Inspiration will be apparent everywhere you look: on paper-handkerchief boxes, in the garden, on · allpaper, in book illustrations – the list is truly limitless, and at this point one must stop talking about one's notions – it can be very wearing for other people!

Even if you are convinced that designing is an activity which you cannot incorporate into an already busy life, it is just as well to know what is involved. Commissioning a professional to prepare a canvas especially for you is marvellously luxurious but hideously expensive, and it is useful to know exactly what to ask for and what to expect. It's terribly frustrating when the result is not *quite* what you had imagined. My disappointments always happened because I had not known how to make my requirements completely clear.

My 'kimona' cushion (shown being stretched) was worked on 12 mesh mono canvas and I used tapestry wool from the WHI. We were able to match the colours pretty accurately, but the design is 'free-handed'.

83

To revert to you. The beginning is the drawing. If you really can't draw, do not despair. You may have noted interesting shapes which can be cut out and arranged and re-arranged until you have a composition which can be pasted on to paper and coloured in, or pinned on and the outlines drawn. You can trace something that pleases – a drawing or a photograph – and then again some designs lend themselves to being drawn 'freehand'. (Don't despise the doodle.) Say you want to make someone a birthday present incorporating initials and a date, you don't even have to buy a stencil kit with an alphabet or numbers 1–10 (though they are fun to play with). Your bookshelf will present you with a huge choice of letters that can be traced and then enlarged to suit the size of canvas you've chosen to use.

Before you decide to make a final, 'clean' drawing, make sure that your paper is the same size as the canvas and very carefully quarter both by making vertical and horizontal lines that cross in the middle, cutting the area to be embroidered and drawn on. This ensures an accurate 'line up'. The paper can be graph paper, which simplifies one's life no end. Find it in rolls in an art shop, or a good stationer's shop. Buy some sheets in a size corresponding to the number of threads per inch on the canvas (e.g. ten squares per inch on graph paper for 10 mesh canvas). When designing on graph paper, quarter it in the same way as you would plain paper.

The drawing can be made directly on to this graph paper; in the case of a geometric design, it is of course much easier to work on graph paper. I was given a present of transparent graph paper which came from America, and it's most convenient to be able to trace directly on to it (but so far I've been unable to find any in London and the firms I called in the provinces had all gone out of business). It is a good idea to keep the original pattern or drawing or photograph by you so that you can refer back to source while sewing. If you made up the design, try colouring it in and keep it for reference, consulting it frequently.

There are several ways of transferring the design to canvas. (I can only just count and I'm as blind as a bat, so it was ages before I could be induced to try this.) If you have worked with cut-out shapes, you can lay them on the canvas in your already decided combinations and tack or draw around the outline.

Another method is to lay a sheet of tracing paper over the design and draw all the outlines in a *very* black marker. When you are tracing, aim at simplifying; leave out fiddly details and bear in mind that when, for example, you are embroidering a brick wall, it is quite enough to suggest the bricks by putting in a few here and there. Concentrate on the outlines of buildings or trees. Animal or human figures look very effective if you get the attitude right; the details can be put in quite sparingly when you are drawing. Don't make any concessions to the fact that the nature of the canvas renders everything geometric: draw a curve as a curve. The sewing itself will take care of the 'stepping'.

Place the tracing paper under the canvas and trace the pattern (which will be visible in the bold black) using an *absolutely* waterproof marker in a lighter colour (black might show through the embroidery). While tracing on to canvas, you should not only outline the main shapes but indicate, however roughly, changes of colour or important blocks of colour shading.

If your graph paper corresponds in size to the canvas you can transfer the design by counting threads and lines. (If you are transferring a geometric design, start

A fine example of a modern geometric design. The cushion belongs to John Bates and was designed by Lillian Delavorias.

Shana Alexander worked these cushions from designs by her friend Mr Inman Cook, who has a lovely shop called Woolworks on Madison Avenue in New York. (Photo by Shana Alexander)

from the middle and work outwards, or confusion is bound to ensue.) It's easier if you weight down paper and canvas (or pin them to a board), lining up the vertical and horizontal lines.

A very accurate result is achieved if you place clear plastic graph paper over the original drawing (whether on drawing paper or graph paper). Line up the two sheets and fix them, then taking coloured markers draw all the colour changes and shading. If you are in doubt when sewing you can check your progress by counting lines and squares.

When drawing on canvas you will find it very annoying when the pen or pencil bumps over the threads and shoots off on a line of its own. This can be obviated by *pulling* gently along the canvas instead of pushing, or holding the pen in an upright position and jerking along.

Although we women have wrested needlepoint back from being an exclusively male preserve, the fact remains that men still produce some of the finest needlework and I wish I had more examples in this book. I am assured that exquisite fine needlepoint has been accomplished in times of war – by Top Brass – in the field . . . I deeply regret that I don't know any major-generals.

One famous actor who shall remain nameless swore his family not to talk of his hobby and was mortified when he absentmindedly opened the door to Coral Browne and realised that he was still holding his needlepoint. It is strange, in view of the enviable pre-eminence of men in haute coûture and other forms of decorative arts, but the fact remains that many men feel embarrassed to display an interest in needlepoint.

My friend Bryn Ellis can turn a hand with ease from carpentry to accounting to painting to needlepoint and has made many lovely things. Almost my favourite is this copy of an antique tile (like Coral's cushion on page 11, an example of good judgement in the choice of art to copy from). The cushion and the tile enhance each other: seeing one at one end of a room, you are moved to look more closely at the other when you come across it. The wool used was tapestry wool on 14 mesh mono canvas. Bryn was also roped in to do one of the pair of gondola cushions (see page 99).

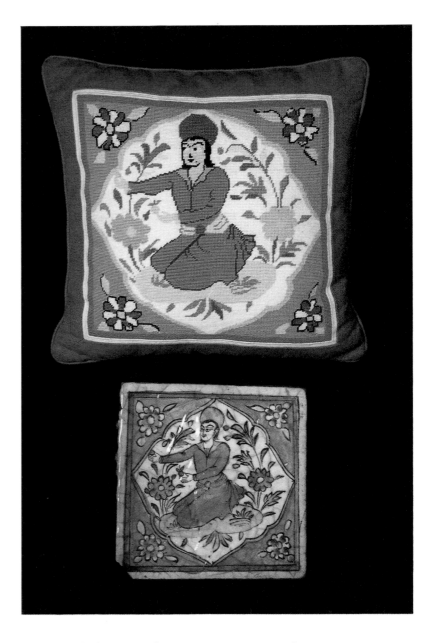

This might be a good moment to suggest that you test your pen to make sure that it is *absolutely* waterproof!

Draw a few lines on a scrap of canvas and hold it under the hot tap – do the worst you can. If there is a hint of smudging, don't use it. If you want to colour the canvas and are going to use markers, check them in the same way.

If you prefer to use paint on the canvas, then oil paints work very well provided they are considerably thinned down with turpentine. If you do decide on oil, it saves a lot of fiddling about if you thin down the colours you intend using and keep them made-up in little jars (like mustard or small honey-pots).

Some acrylic paints run and some don't, so check before buying. Many watercolours can run when damped, but I know people who have never had any trouble with them. Test and check for yourself.

Let the painted canvas dry thoroughly before you start sewing. Don't worry if, when you scrutinise it, the canvas picture looks different from the original (very often the canvas looks awful!). Needlework is bound to, and indeed should, look different from anything else. Even if you are using very fine canvas, some detail is bound to be lost. Accept the fact that you can't get a 'true' curve. It stands to reason that a coarse canvas will reveal the 'steps' to a greater degree than a finer one. This stepped effect can have great charm, of course. The important thing is not to pretend that one isn't *sewing*.

When you are more experienced, there is another method of getting your coloured pattern on to double canvas. After the outlines have been drawn (in mid-brown or grey), take the wools you intend using and fill in the appropriately coloured sections with long horizontal stitches. This is the 'tram' method. Using the same colour wool, stitch over the corresponding trammed colour as though it were painted on. This gives the canvas extra thickness and means you don't have to worry about waterproof pens.

Geometric designs can be sewn directly without being marked, provided you start from the true *centre* and keep counting, referring all the time to your graph paper. When working a Bargello design (*see page 49*), work all of the first line horizontally across the centre of the canvas starting on the right-hand side and moving left.

Repeat above and below following the first lines, and you'll find you no longer have to count. After you have worked a few lines, test your choice of colours in a smallish patch to the side of the design. This is the time to change your mind!

You may find a design that is just right for what you have in mind but to your dismay it is much smaller (or bigger) than you would like it to be. Don't discard it; it can be enlarged or decreased. Trace the pattern (or photograph or painting) on to paper and draw a grid over it, or draw it on to graph paper. If it needs to be twice as big, draw a grid which is twice the size and copy the drawing on to this second grid. When I say copy, I mean count the number of holes each part of the design occupies on the original graph, then count out the same number on the bigger graph and draw that section to fit the space. Make sure the outline is very clearly marked. Place the canvas over the paper (lining up the grid lines and canvas lines) and trace the design on to the canvas.

It may amuse you to read this instruction from *A scholehouse for the needle* by Richard Shorleyker (1624). A specimen page was ruled into squares and accompanied by this: 'I would have you know that the use of these squares doth showe how you may contrive any work, Bird, Beaste or Flower: into bigger or lesser proportion according as you can see the cause: as this if you enlarge your pattern divide it into squares; then rule a paper as large as ye list, into what

Kaffe Fassett designed these slippers for Terence Stamp and they were worked by Terence's Aunt Maud: her first and last piece of needlepoint – a true labour of love . . . The base canvas was white so Terence had it washed in coffee in case the whiteness showed through.

squares you will: then looke how many holes your pattern doth contain, upon so many of the holes of your ruled paper draw your pattern.'

If you find a design that is too big for your canvas, follow the same process in reverse.

A simpler method is to take your over-small or over-large drawing and have it photostatically enlarged or decreased. Photocopying is more expensive than your home effort, but it is absolutely accurate. If you are working from a photograph, it can be reduced or enlarged from the original negative.

Whichever method you employ, the design must be made the exact size you wish the finished embroidery to be.

Other things to note are that you should leave at least 2 inches (5 cm) of plain canvas around the area to be embroidered. Ensure that the selvedge runs from top to bottom and bind the edges with masking tape.

The finished canvas of my first Chinese character.

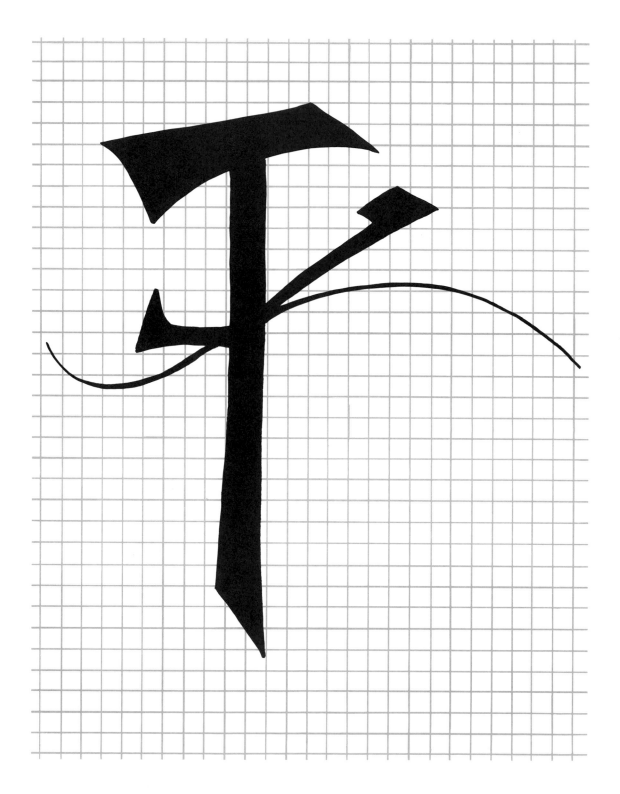

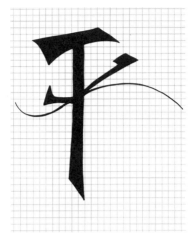

Using graph paper to scale up my Chinese character

Does this still seem confusing? I remember that I didn't really understand the process until I'd struggled through it with a great deal of tearing up and crossing out and gnashing of teeth. I happen to have the drawings of the Chinese character cushion and I'll show them here tidied up by someone else. The originals are nothing to be proud of (I *really* cannot count) and would have helped you only by inducing a justifiable sense of superiority.

Here is a list of materials you might need:

Drawing paper (buy in big sheets that can be cut up)
Tracing paper
Graph paper
Transparent tracing graph paper (if possible)
Clear plastic graph paper (if possible)
Waterproof black marker
Waterproof grey or mid-brown marker
Waterproof coloured markers or *oil paints and turpentine* or *waterproof acrylic paints* or *water colours*
No. 5 sable paint brush
Soft and hard pencils

Some Guidelines on Colour

You may have a natural talent for using colours in which case you don't need to read much of this, but some people who are perfectly capable of decorating a room or buying an outfit will boggle a bit when choosing the colours for something which they have designed, simply because there is no way of telling exactly what the finished result will look like. It's worth knowing a little about which colours work with each other and what some combinations will accomplish for you.

The *primary* colours are *red, yellow* and *blue,* and these three colours when mixed together will give us three more:

> red and yellow give *orange*
> blue and yellow give *green*
> red and blue give *purple*

These are called *complementary* colours, and when these are mixed they give us *tertiary* colours:

> orange and green give (citron) *lemon*
> orange and purple give *russet*
> green and purple give *olive*

This fruit carpet is a bit of a problem . . . About four years ago Frankie and I sat down in the shop in Pimlico Road and picked out fifteen drawings of fruits that would go together and decided on colours that would suit a bedroom that Robin and I were designing in London. Before it was finished (and I did stop and start and stop shamelessly) we moved house and the colours no longer suit. No-one knows where the fruits will finally come to rest.

I used double tapestry wool again and the canvas was Penelope 8 mesh. It is all worked in basketweave.

95

There will be times when you may want to mix strands of colour to achieve subtle shading effects.

There are rooms where one couldn't sit and read a book, clothes that cheer one up, bedrooms that calm one down, colours that look terrific in sunshine but which would look bad on a Scottish moor. Briefly, the fire and sunshine colours – yellow, red, orange and russet – are exciting, hot and cheering. Blue, green and grey are cool, restful colours. All this is probably familiar, but you may not be aware of the effect that colours have on each other. For example if you use a strong aggressive colour like orange or red as a background, the pattern in the foreground will be diminished. Blue or grey or pale green will throw the foreground design forward. It's fascinating to see a pattern change and look quite different because of the background colour on which it is placed. It is quite a good idea to collect pieces of plain, coloured paper along with a basketful of scraps of cotton or silk (the textures will also affect colour). A background of black or white will present the foreground colours absolutely 'true' (every other colour changes neighbouring colours) but black will make the foreground pattern appear smaller than it really is.

Too much subtle shading can make your design dull and vague, and too many bright, contrasting colours can be too demanding on the eye. After a certain point you're really on your own and can only proceed by trial and error. When you are starting, keep your 'inspirational' drawing, or painting, or photograph by you and try and follow the colours which attracted you in the first place.

In the same way that texture changes the character of a colour – the same shade of blue will look different in tweed and muslin – the stitches that you use will alter the appearance of your embroidery yarn.

Basketweave and tent stitch, being closely woven, will intensify the colour and these stitches give a very smooth, bright effect. Any stitch that gives a texture, such as rice stitch or brick stitch, will break up the colour and produce a much lighter effect. This is convenient as the textured stitches are often faster to work and very suitable for background. They also add interest to a large area. The closer stitches are better for use on the actual pattern; tent is best for drawing shapes and a stitch like Gobelin is lovely for filling in sections of pattern.

It is quite important to make your colour decisions before you start stitching. At first, stick to your plan as faithfully as you can but as you become more experienced, remember that all these 'rules' can be broken if it suits your design for you to do so.

In an ideal world, Venice would be my
second home. I have friends, Leslie and
Buzz Bruning, who many years ago had
the wisdom to decide to live there, and
through them I have had access to what I
fondly think of as the 'real' Venice, but I
only go there and I think that living there is
a pre-requisite of really 'knowing' the
Serenisima. Even so, I shall never forget
standing in one of the three remaining
gondola boatyards with a friend, Gino
Macropodio, one of the best gondoliers in
Venice, as a new and very special gondola
was slowly built. The craft was being made
by Nedis Tramontin ('We Tramontins have
only been building boats here for five
hundred years,' he says deprecatingly),
with an oarlock by The Master, Carli, and
sporting a hand-engraved ferro. Were it the
simplest sort of gondola it would still use
the required 280 pieces of wood including
oak, fir, cherry, walnut, mahogany, white
pine, larchwood and lime wood (let no-one
ever complain of the price of a gondola
ride). This boat, I thought, deserves some
hand-made cushions among the brasses,
ribbons and furniture. The cushions were
stealthily drawn up from Gino's tiny grey-
on-grey business card. I kept my fingers
crossed that the little beast in the centre was
indeed intended to be a porcupine, not a
hedgehog. Of course I dawdled and when
delivery time came round I was very busy,
so Bryn Ellis was co-opted as partner. Since
we had only outlines to go on we tried to
match up colours and shading on the
phone. The results are pretty good, but a
needlepointer can spot the differences (and
in fact Bryn's is neater). We took our
precious cushions to Venice personally, and
mild though we are and dog-lovers both, if
those nice Alsatians at the airport had
indicated that the cushions should be torn
apart in the interests of security, there
would have been general mayhem in
Customs and Excise.
(Gondola photo by Leslie Bruning)

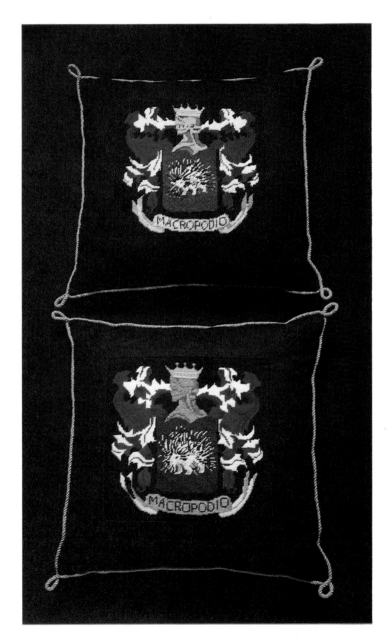

FRAMES OR NOT

Some embroiderers (myself included) never use a frame and, until recently, I hadn't given the matter a thought. When I did think of it the reason was that I had moved house and it came to me that a large standing frame would look rather nice in a space that presented itself near a big window in the sitting room. To be honest I fancied that *I* might look rather nice as part of this set-dressing, prettily seated, two hands flying gracefully the way they do in books, head serenely inclined. It would certainly be a change from sitting cross-legged on the floor or crouched on the arm of a chair, tongue between teeth, spare wool and half-finished canvas clamped under one arm, need I continue?

When I began to look into the means of achieving this arrangement, I was a bit taken aback to realise that it was assumed in some quarters that a frame was a necessity, not at all an alternative or an addition (and certainly not a bit of interior decoration)!

I wouldn't go so far as to say that a frame is a necessity (Millie Rowlands' carpet (*page 110*) was done on her lap and Mary Martin's 'family' rug (*page 72*) was worked in the same way) but I can now see that there are clear advantages.

The main argument against 'framing' is that it's aggravating not to be able to snatch up one's canvas and take off with it at a moment's notice, but upon reflection I realised that there is rarely a moment when I don't have two or more bits of work on the go and I suspect this goes for most ardent embroiderers (and anyone with a low boredom-threshold). It's quite feasible to have one canvas which one works only at home (in the case of a standing frame) or when one is settled for a few hours on a train or in a waiting room (in the case of small, portable frames), and several other smaller pieces for carrying around.

The advantages are that you hardly need to do any blocking or pressing (*see page 108*) on a canvas that has been sewn in a frame; it is easier to maintain a smooth, regular appearance and, of course, it's useful to have both hands free. Counting stitches is easier and this makes geometric work simpler – also if you mark a canvas, say with a pin, it'll stay there and not drift off into the nether regions of the bag along with the bits of wool and spare needles and Kleenex and emery board and mints, the embroiderer's version of the schoolboy's pocket. It's also possible to keep a few needles with different colours in operation and pinned out of the way on the canvas. Mistakes show up earlier on a stretched piece and checking is simpler (and therefore one might check more often and make fewer mistakes).

I have it in mind to embark on a biggish wall-hanging and shall try that in a standing frame. Meanwhile, I have tried a few lap frames, or frames you can prop between yourself and the edge of a table or back of a chair, and though it seems strange at first it doesn't take long to become accustomed to the new method.

KINDS OF FRAMES

The most basic sort of frame is simply four rigid bits
of wood in the shape of a square on to which the
prepared canvas is lashed. (This is best suited to a
smallish canvas.) You may have an old, solid picture
frame and try your hand with that; a friend of mine
made a crude but usable frame from a cut up floor-
mop handle.

If you are using this simplest of frames, the canvas is
prepared by first drawing or tacking a line through
the centre vertically and horizontally. Hem a small
turning all round. Then attach webbing or very strong
tape to the turning on each side, right side of canvas
to right side of webbing. To do this, fix the webbing/
tape to the centre of each side of the canvas and work

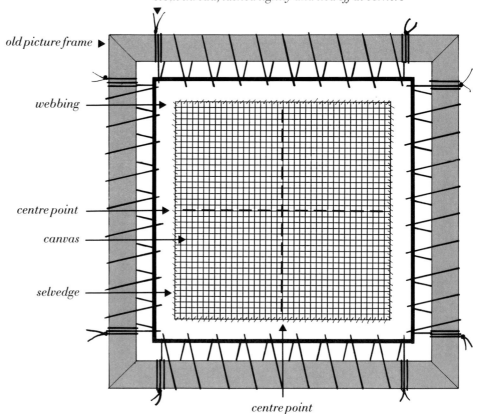

stout thread, lashed tightly and tied off at corners

old picture frame ▶

webbing

centre point

canvas

selvedge

centre point

from the middle to the right and left, and from centre to top and centre to bottom. Having done this, lash the webbing to your home-made frame.

It is important to note that the selvedge should always run vertically in the frame. (This is always the case except when you are working a long narrow object such as a piano stool.)

If you decide to buy a frame you can choose between two kinds: a flat-bar frame or a screw-bar frame (a standing frame would be the screw-bar type). The only difference between them is that the former is tightened with split pins or pegs in the holes of the side pieces, and the latter by using wooden screw rings. Both differ from a fixed frame in that they enable you to work on a piece of canvas which can be much longer than the height of the frame. The canvas is rolled upwards through the frame as it is needed.

The frames usually have webbing already attached, top and bottom. If they do not, then attach the webbing to the top and bottom sides (called the rollers) by means of tin tacks placed at 1 inch (2.5 cm) intervals. Make a ½ inch (1.25 cm) turning at the top and bottom of the canvas. Mark the centre point of each piece of webbing and draw your vertical and horizontal lines through the centre of the canvas. The centre point of the canvas and the centre point of the webbing must be perfectly aligned. Oversew the edges of webbing and canvas, starting at the centre point. Then, starting at the centre again, overcast with really strong thread or string, pulling canvas and webbing taut. Now slot in the side pieces and put in the split pins or the circular screw rings. At this stage the canvas still needs to be extended sideways and in order to do this another piece of webbing (about 1½ inches/3.75 cm wide) must be backstitched to the right and left sides of the canvas and then lashed on to the flat or circular side pieces (starting at the centre and working up, then down from the centre) using very strong thread or string and working at 1 inch (2.5 cm) intervals. Always fix the side webbing on to the canvas after you have fixed it to the rollers and remove it when you have finished that piece of embroidery and before you roll on to the next piece of canvas, as the webbing mustn't be rolled on. Once you are framed up, complete the square in the frame before rolling it on.

If you are making a table runner or a long piano stool, then your sides (and your selvedge) will need to be placed on the rollers, not on the sides of the frame. Be careful to turn the frame before you start working or you'll find yourself stitching in the wrong direction. (Needless to say, you can't turn a standing frame, so this sort of work requires a 'hand' or 'lap' frame.)

Your canvas will look like this when it is framed upon a screw pin frame.

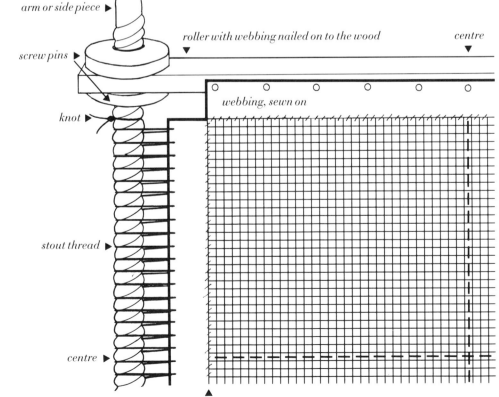

arm or side piece ▶

screw pins ▶

knot ▶

stout thread ▶

centre ▶

roller with webbing nailed on to the wood

centre ▼

webbing, sewn on

▲ selvedge of canvas runs vertically

If you are working a long canvas, the unsewn part is at the bottom and the embroidered part moves upwards on to the top roller.

I have now seen a standing frame in a friend's sitting-room; it *is* a pretty bit of décor and the work in progress attracts a good deal of ego-soothing comment, I notice . . .

Shows are remembered for wildly different reasons: the one where I had tooth-ache for the whole run; the one in which I was rather bad and made a lot of money; the one in which I was frightfully good and lost my shirt. Gigi is the show in which I met and made friends with one of my heroines, Beryl Reid. We played sisters, which was a bit of a laugh for a start, and we have rarely stopped laughing since we met. We're pictured on stage laughing – or is it singing?

Beryl adores cats and has infinite patience with their moods and illnesses. I made her a little pillow of a cat looking safe. It is partly basketweave and partly half-cross stitch. It was worked in two strands of Persian yarn on 12 mesh mono canvas. (The nose was unpicked a good deal.) This was my first stab at grading colours and is not totally successful. Beryl says she doesn't mind . . . (Gigi photo by Zoë Dominic)

FINISHING

BLOCKING OR STRETCHING

If you have worked your canvas without a frame and if you have been using a diagonal stitch (tent, for example), then the finished work will be lozenge-shaped instead of rectangular. As time goes by and your feeling for the tension becomes keener, the lozenge will be much less pronounced, but the canvas will still be a bit out of shape and in need of stretching (or blocking, as it is sometimes called).

Get yourself a piece of chip-board or cork or an old drawing board, and make sure it is clean. (Plywood is a bit too tough.) Then lay on the wood a piece of clean white cloth or a couple of sheets of blotting paper. Pin to the board with drawing pins or small tin-tacks (don't bang them all the way in).

At this point the reverse side of the canvas should be slightly dampened, also the cloth or absorbent paper on the board.

Pin the canvas, right side up, to the board, lining up the selvedge and the left-hand edge of the board. Pull it taut and tack it (through the unworked part) at 1 inch (2.5 cm) intervals to the very corners of the canvas. Then stretch either the top or bottom side at right angles (use the top or bottom of the board or check the angle with a T-square or set-square). Pull into place and tack the canvas as before. Now you can take a ruler and draw in the correct line for the other two sides. (If you prefer, you can draw the square on to the paper or fabric before you start and follow your own line. If you do this, the canvas can be pinned anywhere on the board.) Now pull and stretch the two sides until they exactly fit into the square shape. Leave for twenty-four hours, at the end of which the canvas should be dry and back to its original shape.

If you are handling a very thick, heavy duty canvas, you should pin it to the board on and just inside the worked section, not through the bare canvas which might not be able to stand up to the strain and would break. Be careful to put the tacks or pins alongside the stitches, not through the yarn where you might damage it. Canvas embroidery is very hard-wearing so don't be afraid of stretching it.

At this point you can take it to the framer or the upholsterer, both of whom will do your stretching for you if you prefer. Stretching is included in the price of framing and upholstering, so if you have done that bit of work at home, make sure that the stretching charge is deducted!

MOUNTING

Even if your canvas is to be professionally framed, you can save money by mounting it at home.

Buy a piece of hardboard or plywood which is exactly the size of your embroidery, and lay the canvas on it, right side up. You can put in a few pins to hold the canvas in place while you turn the board over and

Millie Rowlands is more adventurous than I am and here is a picture of her drawing-room hearth-rug photographed in the Rowlands' country house. It took four years to complete and had to be left in the bedroom because it was too heavy to carry about.

Millie reckons that her right-to-left, then left-to-right cross-stitching provides a good thickness of wool on the surface and has proved very hard-wearing. There was no 'design' as such. She threw down a handful of leaves and made a note of where they landed (rather like the best method of planting bulbs). She decided where the light should be seen to come from so that the shadowing was consistent, and worked the leaves before applying the veining and imposing the stems.

The carpet is worked on double canvas, 12/24 mesh. There is a large centre piece three feet wide, and two small side pieces. The whole is nine feet by seven feet. The wool is crewel wool from the Royal School of Neeedlework (and the canvas was also stretched, pressed and backed by them) and a local upholsterer sewed the carpet to the fitted carpet.

glue down the bare borders of the canvas. (If the embroidery is fairly small and light, it's enough to lace the canvas across the back.)

Embroidery looks better framed without glass, so you can, if you wish, spray it with protective Scotch-guard at this point.

JOINING

You may need to join pieces of canvas before sending them off to an upholsterer. If the join is not meant to show, for example if you have been obliged to work a large object in sections because of the width of the canvas available, then this is how you proceed. As you sew, leave about seven or eight threads unworked at the end of each row on the side which is to be joined, and leave some working threads hanging. Make a turning in the raw canvas (still leaving unworked canvas on the 'right' side). Line up the sides to be joined in such a way that two verticals meet – these will henceforth be treated as one vertical. Using stout thread, join the two pieces of canvas, oversewing and using the same colour thread as the base canvas colour. Then take the hanging threads and continue embroidering over the joined canvas.

If you haven't left hanging threads, take new wool and cast on as usual.

Be careful not to embroider through the turned-back canvas as this can form a ridge. Press the canvas at the back, back against its own side after you have finished joining up. This process can be repeated indefinitely. If you have lots of bits, join them up along the horizontal sides until you have long strips. Then join the strips together. (Millie Rowland's carpet (*page 110*) is in three strips.)

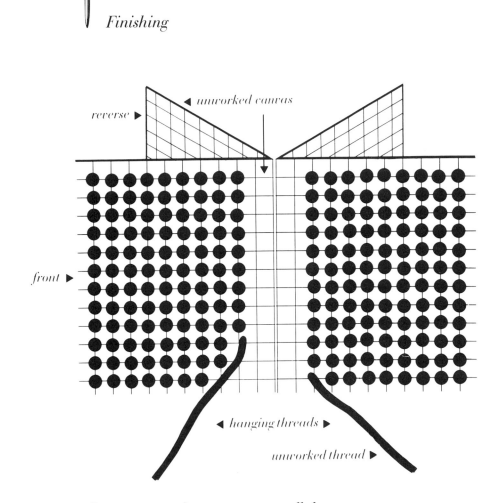

reverse ▶ ◀ *unworked canvas*

front ▶

◀ *hanging threads* ▶

unworked thread ▶

In some cases it matters not at all that one can see where the joins happen – in fact that may be part of the design and the part to be joined may have been outlined in a border colour – but one mustn't see a smidge of bare canvas. Simply fold back the bare canvas, lining up the threads very carefully. Join the pieces with strong button thread taken under the creased edge and only just above the embroidery, so that you draw the embroidered edges together without showing any canvas at all. Press lightly on the wrong side.

Making a Cushion

I sew so badly that I am very reluctant to finish anything off at home (and anyway a professional finish makes things look better than they are in reality

These shell cushions started out as the first squares of a carpet for a house in the west of Ireland but I was daunted by the prospect of fifteen squares in 12 mesh with this dark green background, so the seaside carpet became a pair of inner city cushions.

OPPOSITE: *We have what was to have been a wall of shame – all flops; our own and really spectacular ones by close friends. Unfortunately some successes crept in and the impact is somewhat diminished. On the couch is a jumble of cushions (again, some less successful than others). The Staffordshire china figures are a WHI design and are the very first canvases I attempted, so I'm especially fond of them. The larger, brown Bargello is wrong because I didn't work it out beforehand, nor did I count from the centre of the canvas. The 'R' is for my husband Robin and I do initial cushions on a fairly regular basis.*

and that's always a good thing). I am however assured that putting a cushion together is something that almost anyone who isn't me will find pretty simple.

I rather favour cushions that simply overlap at the back so that the pad can be removed and the cover cleaned without unpicking and sewing. The material for the back has to have an overlap of about 4 inches (10 cm) and this means that you should allow an extra 8 inches (20 cm) above the length of the embroidered side, plus a bit of turning on both sections of back. Having cut the material into two, make a little turning on both halves and press, then fold back 2 inches (5 cm) on each half and stitch. Overlap the two pieces so that they fit the required area and pin and tack them. Place the front and back

together with right sides facing. Tack them and hand or machine stitch taking the stitching line through the last holes taken up by the embroidery so that no bare canvas is seen.

If you prefer a closed cushion, sew three sides on the wrong side, turn the right way out, insert the pad and slip stitch the fourth side.

There are many ways of prettying up cushions – adding frills and double frills, braid and bands of fabric around the embroidered front, and cords; those of you who can sew well will know better than I how to achieve these effects, and those of us that can't can take comfort in the fact that canvas embroidery looks marvellous even if the making-up is plain as plain.

Putting Things Right

Removing Stains

It stands to reason that I do a great deal of sewing in time which belongs to my employer of that moment. It's standard to be dismissed for a couple of hours to one's dressing-room (theatre or studio) or to an orange box in the lee of a friendly catering van (location filming), and the moment the wig is off and the coffee is on and the canvas nicely under way, all-high changes its mind, the performing dogs are dismissed and one is urgently needed on the set. I loathe keeping people waiting in any circumstances and can fling myself into wig and make-up with a speed that baffles the eye, but alas, the first thing that gets tossed into a corner is whatever is on my lap. That is usually a book, a canvas and a handful of wool, so you can imagine the variety of stains with which my dresser and I have had to cope (I think the worst was face oil; one of those with unspecified, magical properties that make you look ten years younger). Then again, at home there are the cats . . . Burmese cats seem to have perfected a way of travelling very fast with feet scarcely touching the ground until they reach a familiar bit of embroidery: muddy garden to the Bargello in one. They also stamp about a lot on the hearthrugs, and one of them,

Spencer, who has turned 'marking' into a complex means of communication – well, I draw a veil.

Things happen: people spill wine, candles drip, ceilings leak. A super dry-cleaner can fix almost anything but this does cost an arm and five legs, so here are my findings after many an accident.

It is amazing how effective soap and water can be. I was terrified the first time I washed a piece of embroidery, but this is how I got off grease-based make-up, and I think this applies for any grease spot. Simply wash in warm (not hot) soapy water, then go to work with alcohol or alcohol-based spot remover. The trick is to go cautiously. Coffee or tea stains can also be washed, and a friend of mine then rinses by pouring clear hot water through the canvas.

Animal disasters are fairly simple. Mud, when dry, brushes off and rarely leaves a stain. Misdemeanours should be sprayed with soda water and then dabbed gently with a clean, dry cloth or sponge.

Wine stains should be sprinkled with salt and 'dabbed in' with a damp cloth, then left for a few hours and rinsed with hot water and lemon juice.

I was once so engrossed in a television programme that, trying to watch and sew, I stabbed my finger and then a *really* exciting bit started and I couldn't look down and by the time I did I saw that I had bled over a nice bit of ivory background. It was late at night so I just did what one does to a piece of cloth, rinsed it in cold water to get most of the blood out, then rinsed in warm, soapy water, then rinsed in clear cold water. Start with cold and end with cold.

I'm told, though I haven't tried it, that the usual procedure for getting ink out of a tablecloth will also remove ink from a piece of embroidery. First apply milk and keep doing this until most of the ink is out. Then dab at the stain with a damp cloth or sponge which has been dipped in lemon juice (or salt). Let it dry naturally, then, if necessary, give it a warm, soapy wash. My dresser once got a lipstick smear off by gently rubbing with vaseline and then washing carefully in warm, soapy water.

Here's a smart remedy which I learned the other day for removing candle-wax. As someone else's bad luck had it, I had the chance of trying it out almost at once on a Christmas sweater, 'out' for the first time. It worked. Take an ice cube and apply to the wax. This makes it hard and brittle and easy to scrape or pick off. Put the canvas (or sweater) between two slightly damp towels or two bits of blotting paper and press with a warm iron.

It can happen that a bit of yarn or cotton or silk in a piece of embroidery is not colour fast, and it's horrible to realise as you wash something that one colour is running all over the place, but the situation can be saved. Put the embroidery in cold water and keep changing the water until the stain is out. This can take ages, maybe two days, but it should work if you keep at it long enough.

Almost everything can be put right.

UNPICKING STITCHES AND MENDING CANVAS

It may happen that you just have to unpick a section of work. When I came to stitch my drawing of Beryl's cat it looked a bit peculiar, whereas the drawing had looked all right. When the background was done the cat looked even worse. My husband looked at it and said, 'Why have you done Beryl a fox, and why is it grey?' What had happened, I think, was that I had gone well over the outline of the muzzle into the background area and maybe a line drawing on paper didn't reveal that the snout was too sharp in the first place. I unpicked a little piece and re-stitched and it was still wrong, so I unpicked a bigger area and changed the profile altogether and that seemed to do it, and I learned a bit about *unpicking*. If you catch a mistake in time you can unpick a small area using the needle and getting the stitches out one by one, but if you're dealing with bigger area with maybe a horizontal pattern which is nudging some diagonally worked background or surrounded by a totally different stitch and there's a lot of casting on and casting off, there's nothing for it but to cut out a whole patch of stitches. Although this can be done from the front I feel safer dealing with the cutting on the reverse side (use very small, fine scissors). When you are clear of the section which you need to re-sew, go to work with your needle unpicking more stitches and making sure that no small cut ends remain which will unpick themselves later on. When you have about ¾ in (2 cm) of yarn hanging from each unpicked row, lay the ends across the blank, unpicked area on the wrong side and make sure that you stitch over them when you re-sew.

It's a heart-stopping moment when you realise that you've cut into the canvas. This happened to me while I was unpicking a piece of black background on a 'Gondola' cushion. I'd done two silly things: a diagonal row of basketweave had been completed and cast off and the thread woven in. Instead of looking at the reverse side, I thought I remembered completing a 'down' line, and in fact I'd last done an 'up' line. It's always better to leave off in the middle of a row and to check the back. 'Up' stitches do actually go up like steps ＿=ˉand 'down' stitches point down ˡₗₗ. (Well, they don't actually point, but it's a way of

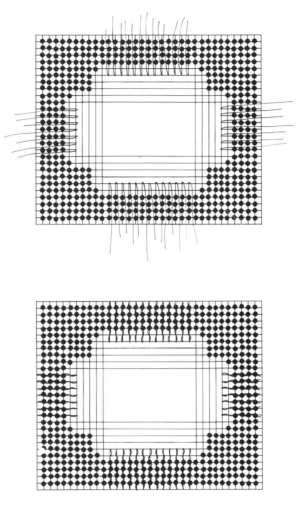

The hole, tidied up and showing canvas threads unpicked and ready for threading

The canvas; unpicked threads woven back into the embroidery

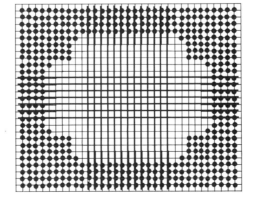

The heavy lines show new canvas thread darning the hole

remembering.) Even on the black background I could detect a faint ridge where I'd done two 'up' rows together and crossly and hurriedly unpicking the row, I nicked into the canvas. The *mend* is quite undetectable and very secure.

Turn to the reverse of the canvas. The area around the break or hole has to be cleared of sewn stitches, and the cut canvas thread or threads unwoven until there is enough free canvas thread to be threaded into a needle (you only need about ¾ inch (2 cm). Hold the eye near to the thread) and woven back into the embroidery. Take some canvas thread from the very edge (or from another similar-sized canvas), thread it and weave into the wrong side of the stitching, then go on and darn the hole, making new canvas. (It's easier than real darning.) Stitch normally over your darn.

If by some chance you cut a canvas which has not been sewn the process is slightly different. If you know what colour and what stitch will eventually cover the damaged part, work that stitch around the hole leaving ¾ inch (2 cm) of clear canvas, then proceed as above. If the area will have pattern on it, leave blank then further unpick the broken canvas threads to make the hole neat and easy to deal with. Take new canvas thread, knot it and with a needle bring it through from the front to the reverse. Darn the hole from at least ¾ inch (2 cm) away. Leave until you come to stitch, then when you are working, sew over the hanging ends and after sewing cut off the knots on the right side of the work.

Appendix

Sew in a good light. I don't observe this rule when I'm away from home and will sew anywhere so long as I can more or less see the canvas. Nearly always I regret this. I have unpicked tracts of blue background which should have been green (try not to sew greens at all unless you're in daylight or really good artificial light), and I've also had to unpick horrible, 'bumpy' work. I've purposely not yet unpicked the second square down on my 'stitches sampler' (*see page 59*) which was done on a train, at night and is a disgrace.

I was lucky enough to meet Mary Martin when she came to London to launch a range of bed-linen which she had designed. I told her how much I had enjoyed her book and how much I admired the little pillow with its posy of violets which she had made for her adored mother-in-law. 'Ah yes,' she said pensively, 'that was the one I went blind doing.' She was exaggerating but it seems that the intricate flowers did take their toll.

If you are uncomfortable, squinting and frowning, don't be vain, use a magnifier. It is such a joy to be able to see properly. I use several kinds.

When I am working on, say, a carpet which is pretty coarse I keep a hand magnifier by me and use it for *checking* bits and pieces.

When I am working on anything from 12 mesh to 18 mesh (I don't go much smaller) I wear a magnifier which hangs around my neck, looks like a large piece of costume jewellery when not in use and is propped on my chest when needed so it projects between my face and the needlework on my lap.

At home, I also have a small standing magnifier. Placed on the table it enables me to look through it at the work below on the table, but it is on the small side. (A few months ago I saw a *wonderful* standing model in a needlework shop. The assistant sympathetically damped down my enthusiasm and explained that they hardly ever stocked them because so few were sold. Not surprising. The really super ones are nearly £200 each. If you're incredibly rich, or are due for a special present . . .) However, the round-the-neck model is easily obtainable and is very modestly priced. Cautionary note: it is very tempting to use this magnifier when sitting up in bed watching television (which is only intermittently gripping). If you sink down into the pillows, then turn suddenly to talk to someone or pick up scissors, the pain when the magnifier falls back on you and strikes the small area between your upper lip and your nostrils is hateful. Just try and remember that it is there.

In a good light and helped by a magnifier, your brow should be calm and unfurrowed. If, however, you feel yourself getting into a frenzy over something that keeps going wrong, remember that your face is getting into a frenzy too. What you do is stick a piece of strong elastoplast or sellotape between your eyebrows or, even better, persuade an American friend to send you some Frownies: little bits of gummed paper which when pasted between the brows remind you not to frown. Believe me it will only take callers at the door a matter of weeks to become accustomed to your strange appearance when, embroidery in hand, you absent-mindedly open the door with a bit of brown paper stuck on your face . . .

ACKNOWLEDGEMENTS

Special thanks to Frankie Salter at the Women's Home Industries shop in Pimlico Road, London SW1, who taught me a lot as I went along.

Thanks also to Eleanor Summerfield, Toffee Hingston, Pat O'Toole, Heather Shell and Jan Rowl for helping with background sewing; Joanne Rice for assembling and sewing the needlecase and helping with carpet borders; Bryn Ellis for sewing one of the gondola cushions, painted by the WHI from a design supplied by me; Jill Batty, who deciphered my writing and typed the manuscript; and all my kind friends who sent me photographs or allowed us to photograph their work.

The fruit carpet was drawn up in my colours by the WHI and assembled and backed by the Royal School of Needlework, Princes Gate, London SW7.

USEFUL BOOKS

Joan Edwards
Small Book on the History of Embroidery
(Batsford)

Lanio Synge
R.S.N. Book of Needlework & Embroidery
(Collins)

April Colby
Samplers
(Batsford)

Roy Strong & Julia Trevelyan Oman
Elizabeth R
(Secker & Warburg)

V & A Colour Books
Ornate Wallpapers
(Victoria & Albert Museum)

Joan Nicholson
Simple Canvaswork
(Batsford)

Joan Fisher
The Creative Art of Needlepoint Tapestry
(Hamlyn)

Alexander Speltz
The Styles of Ornament
(The Dover Press)

Roy Gender
Growing Old Fashioned Flowers
(David & Charles)

Sylvia Green
Canvas Embroidery for Beginners

Mary Martin
Needlepoint
(Morrow)

Sylvia Sidney
Needlepoint Book
(Reinhold)

Pamela Clayburn
Samplers
(Shire Album)

INDEX

Basket-weave stitch *35*
Bargello stitch *47*
Bates, John *68*
Berlin work *22*
Bess of Hardwick *18*
Blocking *30, 101, 108*
Brick stitch *20, 42*
Browne, Coral *12*
Byzantine stitch *46*

Canvas *28, 29*
  Mono *28, 52*
  Penelope *28, 29*
Cashmere stitch *44, 45*
Colour *95–9*
Continental stitch *35*
Coward, Noel *73*
Cross stitch *14, 20, 47, 57, 65*

Dench, Judi *71*

Encroaching Gobelin stitch *41*
Enlarging *89*

Frames *100, 102*
  Flat-bar *103*
  Screw-bar *103*
  Standing *100*

Gobelin stitch *40*
Graph paper *84*
Greek Cross stitch *47*

Half-cross stitch *14, 35*
Hall, Stanley *72*
Hatton Garden Wall Hangings

Irman, John *69*

Joining canvas *112*

Kean, Marie *9*
Keith, Penelope *78, 79*

La Plante, Lynda *75*
Left-handed needlepoint *53–6*
Lépé, Manuel *68*
Leviathan (Smyrna) Cross stitch *48, 49*
Lohr, Marie *11*
Lucas, George *81*

Mangano, Silvana *9*
Martin, Mary *69, 72, 100, 123*
Mending *119*
Mosaic stitch *43*
Mounting *109*

Needles *31*
New Arts and Crafts Movement *24*

Oil paint *88*
Opus Anglicanum *15*

Pal Joey *67, 68*
Parisian stitch *43*
Pesel, Louisa *65*

Reid, Beryl *78, 107, 119*
Rice stitch *20, 49*
Rowlands, Millie *100*

Samplers *57*
Scottish stitch *44, 45*
Sidney, Sylvia *69*
Slanted Gobelin stitch *40*
Stains *117*
Stamp, Terence *10, 90*
Summerfield, Eleanor *9, 53*
Syon Cope *15*

Tent stitch *14, 20, 35*
Tudor period *16, 17–20*

Warp *14*
Waterproof pens *85*
Women's Home Industries *12, 75*
Woof *14*

Yarn *32*
  Persian *32*
  Tapestry *32*
  Crewel *32*